DEATH OF A
GOOD WOMAN

By Marjorie Eccles

Death of a Good Woman
Cast a Cold Eye

(As Judith Bordill)
The Clouded Mirror
A Candle for Lydia

(As Jennifer Hyde)
Hill of the Caves
Handful of Shadows
Arabesque of Daisies
Winter Magic
A Secret Shore

DEATH OF A GOOD WOMAN

MARJORIE ECCLES

A CRIME CLUB BOOK
Doubleday
NEW YORK   LONDON   TORONTO   SYDNEY   AUCKLAND

All of the characters in this book are fictitious,
and any resemblance to actual persons, living or
dead, is purely coincidental.

A Crime Club Book
Published by Doubleday, a division of
Bantam Doubleday Dell Publishing Group, Inc.
666 Fifth Avenue, New York, New York 10103

Doubleday and the portrayal of a man
with a gun are trademarks of
Doubleday, a division of Bantam Doubleday Dell
Publishing Group, Inc.

Library of Congress Cataloging-in-Publication Data

Eccles, Marjorie.
Death of a good woman / Marjorie Eccles. — 1st ed.
p.   cm.
"A Crime Club book."
I. Title.
PR6055.C33D44   1989
823'.914—dc19   88-21928
                                                        CIP

DEATH OF A
GOOD WOMAN

1

The Saturday before Christmas, with only one more shopping day to go, had been no busier than any other Saturday. The majority of the population of Lavenstock, it seemed, was no more inclined to buy antiquarian books, even at Christmas, than it ever had been, but since he hadn't expected they would be, Edwin wasn't unduly disappointed. One or two small transactions, an old map, and a few orders sent by post had, in fact, been the total extent of his business that week.

Maybe he should have listened to Fleur's suggestions. Her flair for making money was, like her imagination, never in short supply.

For as long as he could remember, the business had only barely paid its way, but as even the least discerning customer was bound to realise some time, that wasn't what Edwin Saville was in it for. His pleasure and passion was to obtain, handle, and only as a last resort sell, rare and beautiful old books.

It was nearly half past four, dark and bitterly raw, and today—this turbulent, calamitous day—unable to shake off that plunging sense of disaster, he couldn't bring himself to hang about any longer, not just on the unlikely chance that the odd customer might conceivably drop in during the next hour. He'd had more than enough for anyone. And he had, after all, a compelling reason for being home early tonight.

Pulling the shop door behind him, he stepped out into the cobblestoned alley half hidden behind the Cornmarket. Strains of "O Come All Ye Faithful" drifted across to him from the Salvation Army band. A street lamp fifty yards away cast a glancing light on the old bow window and the faded sign, EDWIN SAVILLE, ANTIQUAR-

IAN BOOKS, MAPS, PRINTS, the sign that hadn't needed to be changed since his father's time, because he bore the same name.

"Straight out of Dickens, darling!" Fleur would tease, gently smiling, and wasn't he lucky, because that was just what people went for nowadays. He really ought to have the shopfront re-painted, though—shiny black or dark green—and the signboard relettered in gold copperplate or Gothic script. She urged him to leave the blinds up at night as well, with one of his old maps displayed on an easel, lit by a lamp left burning in the window, like the fashionable interior decorator's which had opened on the corner. And while he was at it, why not diversify?

Edwin, seeing another colourful flight of fancy beginning to take wing, and already bored with a proposition he found irrelevant, had pointed out that his father had diversified when he went in for selling prints and maps. He considered he himself had gone far enough by starting a sideline in books on criminology amongst the first editions and other rarities, after his father had died.

"Darling Edwin, the world's changed in twenty-five years!"

And not for the better, he thought as she went on—about selling new books as well as old—and what about those mass-produced prints, already framed? Victorian style for choice, though Art Nouveau and even Art Deco were popular in some quarters. They were going like a bomb; the fashion had gone back to having pic-tures and knick-knacks about the place . . . "You're not listening, are you, Edwin?"

He knew, with an obscure feeling of guilt, that he sometimes got on her nerves, though she'd never actually said so. He wasn't quick or interesting enough for her. But on that occasion he had been listening and prepared to believe what she was saying, though quite unaware himself of this or any other fashion. If people *wanted* reproductions—her short, blunt-tipped little fingers lovingly stroked her own genuine seventeenth-century Pembroke table— what was wrong with supplying them? She was sweet and reason-able, as always, in the way that so few people could resist, certainly not Edwin.

Only this particular idea he'd pushed away, refusing to think of it. Himself, he would rather do without than go for second best, and he couldn't begin to understand how anyone else could feel differently. He'd held this point of view since it had been inculcated into him by his father, and Edwin rarely changed his opinions, once formed. Though to be strictly honest, denial of anything, the pictures and books he loved, not to mention other material comforts, had never needed to feature much in his calculations. He sometimes felt vaguely guilty about this, though not enough to compel him to do anything about it.

As he turned the key in the lock, the half-forgotten conversation with his wife came back to him with sudden, vivid clarity, and he stood for a moment in the lamplight, his long, serious face gaunt. Then he turned away, a tall man in his fifties, raincoated, stoop-shouldered, and thin, his greying, curly hair brushed into the sideways quiff he'd always worn. Carrying the bulky parcel under his arm, he made his way through the square, past the carol-playing band and alongside the market stalls, moving with the absent-minded, sloping stride of a man whose thoughts are habitually turned inwards. Intermittently throughout the afternoon it had sleeted, and the light spilling from the surrounding shops and stalls shone on the layer of thin black mud trampled onto the pavements by the shopping crowds. The big decorated Christmas tree stood, as it did every year, in front of the horse-trough in the centre of the Cornmarket, glowing with coloured lights. There was a strong smell of celery and sprouts and oranges from the greengrocery stalls, and hamburgers and onion from McDonald's across the way.

"Yoo-hoo, Mr. Saville!"

Someone was rattling a collecting tin under his nose. He blinked and saw a familiar face in an unfamiliar frame. Lola Tennyson in her Salvation Army bonnet. The bleached, ragged hair was more or less concealed by the hard straw hat; her meagre figure was encased to the neck in blue serge, but even on Christian duty bent, Lola hadn't been able to resist hitching up her skirt above the knee, a length still mistakenly favoured by her at forty, though why was not easy to understand. Her legs were regrettable, knobbly and sparrow-like. The bonnet was unkind to her thin little face, perky and streetwise, looking always starved and ill-nourished, stamped by generations of underprivilege.

She sounded breathless. "Oh, I'm really glad to see you!"

Edwin's expression registered no reciprocal pleasure at this unexpected and unwanted declaration. "Oh?"

"I left my money on the kitchen table this morning, see, after Mrs. Saville gave it me—did you find it? I tried to get in touch, but—"

"How much?" he interrupted, reaching for his wallet.

"She did give me fifteen, seeing as how I come in special. Oh, that's good of you—save me a lot of trouble, that will; I'd have come up to the house tonight for it, but now—oh, thanks ever so!" The notes he gave her disappeared with a conjurer's dexterity into her pocket. "And I'm sure you'll be pleased to give generously to the Lord's work at this festive season."

She was incredible. Affronted both by the glibness of the spiel and the extremeness of her sudden commitment to yet another craze—Lola could never do anything by halves—only surprised that she wasn't actually clashing cymbals in the band, he tried to tell himself that she probably meant well, that her intentions were as good and genuine as those of her companions. That it was ridiculous to feel a hidden threat under the request, that the gooseberry eyes were looking at him with secret knowledge. Feeling hunted, he thrust another five-pound note into her tin, buying his escape. "God bless you!" followed him, mocking and derisive to his ears.

"Here, watch it, mate!"

Edwin, whose preoccupations quite often made him clumsy and unheeding, had this time blundered against a hardware stall, knocking into a precarious pile of plastic washing-up bowls and baking tins, which the stallholder only just saved with an adroit movement. Stepping back with a muffled apology, his face came into unpleasing contact with the warm and sticky, chocolate-coated hand of a baby being carried in its mother's arms. He fled.

A few minutes' rapid walk and it was all, thank God, left behind —everything he hated: the noise, the crowds, the relentless jollity of these commercialised Christmases. Quiet engulfed him. He strode on in the cold, intense dark, down the hill past the parish church and the park entrance and into Kelsey Road, sheltered and tree-lined, presently reaching the peaceful refuge of his own house, comfortably detached from its neighbours. By then, it had begun to snow in earnest, and looked likely to stick.

The house was in darkness. No welcoming light in the porch to help him with his key in the latch, no curtains drawn back to reveal the warm lamplight of Fleur's tasteful interior, with its Sanderson chintz covers and copper bowls of chrysanthemums, silver photo frames, and the rest. He tried to remember whether she'd said she would be out—she often was, on one of her charitable occasions, though rarely on a Saturday evening. He recalled belatedly it had been the Buttercup Club Christmas party for the children today. That was something he oughtn't to have allowed himself to forget. He stared round dully.

Nothing was left ready—neither his slippers warming nor the usual daintily laid tray on the working surface, with a note to say that there was a casserole on low, salad in the fridge, or a meal he might heat up in the microwave oven. She'd never been forgetful of things like that . . . but then, everyone who knew her agreed what a caring person she was.

He hadn't been able to eat any lunch at all, and now, suddenly, he was ravenously hungry. He felt a need for something filling, satisfying, and soothing. The large fridge was even better stocked than usual in preparation for Christmas, but mostly with raw ingredients as yet, and he was very much afraid he was going to have to cook for himself. Poking about, he came across a bowl of pork dripping on a shelf, poured off from the joint they'd had on Sunday—ready to give to Lola Tennyson, no doubt, who couldn't afford to be as fussy as Fleur about not eating animal fats.

For a moment he hesitated. Well, Fleur wasn't here to see. Experiencing a guilty kind of freedom, Edwin softened the dripping slightly with a quick go in the microwave, then spread it liberally onto several thick, unhandily cut slices of Fleur's home-made wholemeal bread, garnishing it with beads of salty brown jelly from the bottom of the bowl. He softened the dripping further, so that when it set, it would be level again, then carried the food on a tray with a large pot of strong tea and one of the kitchen mugs, into the sitting room.

With the coals in the grate well alight, easy with his jacket off and his old pullover on, settled in his comfortable wing chair with the firelight flickering on silver and gilt and flowers, on his pictures and the soft leather bindings of his books, Edwin settled down to enjoy the illicit schoolboy snack, nostalgically reminiscent of wartime prep-school suppers, bath nights, and his Nana. All that was missing was the cocoa.

"That's incredible!" Nell Fennimore burst out, replacing the telephone before joining her husband in the living room. "I don't believe it—he says she's gone to the cottage, to try and finish her book! *I* didn't know her book was anywhere near finished."

"Fleur Saville's whole life doesn't have to be on open record, not even to you, darling," Gerald answered absently, in the middle of two down and nine across in the *Times*.

"Well, I know, but she *is* my best friend." Nell flushed a little at Gerald's quizzically raised eyebrow, suddenly aware of sounding exactly as she had when she and Fleur had been in the sixth form together at Princess Mary's, when Fleur had already become as graceful and beautiful as she was now, and Nell had been so proud of being her chosen friend. "But he sounded really funny."

"Funny, how?" Gerald abandoned his crossword with resignation. When Nell got these premonitions, there was no shrugging the matter off. She'd go on worrying until everything was settled to her satisfaction. Gerald sighed, but without rancour. Her energetic concern for other people's welfare was, after all, one of the chief reasons he loved her.

"I don't know," she answered, frowning, "just—off. Rather sharp. Not a bit like Edwin, really."

"Probably not very keen at being left to fend for himself. You know how fond of his creature comforts he is."

"That's just it—I've always said Fleur spoils him, and now—it's perfectly ridiculous; he says she may even be away over Christmas!" The last words were uttered with mounting disbelief.

"Good Lord." Even Gerald was surprised at that—but not prepared to let it spoil their Saturday evening. "Come and have a drink, my love," he said, "and forget Fleur for once." Nell hesitated, then smiled faintly.

"I expect you're right. All the same, I think she might have let me know, at least. I had all the organising and most of the clearing-up to see to at the party this afternoon. It's not like her; she's so efficient, and I'd have thought she couldn't have borne not to see how things turned out . . . considering how much it means to her . . . and she's worked so *hard* to make sure everything went smoothly."

"You haven't done so badly yourself, love." Fleur couldn't have had all that much to do, not with the amount of work Nell had put in. She looked worn-out this evening.

"She did have that bad attack a few days ago, remember—somebody had to take over."

"Quite." The subject of Fleur's asthma was one Gerald was liable to grow tired of very easily.

"We shall have to see what we can do about having him here over Christmas as much as possible if she persists in this mad idea of staying up there at the cottage," Nell went on, still troubled.

Gerald suppressed a groan. Edwin was all very well, a good chap, one of the best, really, but so damned—distant. Quite out of this world, sometimes. And Christmas was Christmas, after all. The grandchildren would be staying, and Edwin was hardly likely to be a wow with the tinies.

The trouble with Nell was that she was too good-natured.

She came behind his chair and, leaning over his shoulder, put her cheek against his. "Methuselah," she said, pointing. " 'The mule has thrown the old man.' "

The trouble with her also, you forgot how clever she could be.

By seven o'clock, stamping snow off his boots and closing the door for the last time, Edwin's euphoria had left him. The sad, bitter unease had settled on him again. No Fleur, and the anticipated joy in opening his parcel of books and savouring the contents was quite gone. And perhaps the bread-and-dripping had been a mistake. The fire was almost out, and after he'd mended it from the replenished coal scuttle, feeling stiff and cold, he crossed to draw the heavy velvet curtains against the snow-filled darkness outside. He stood looking out, his hand still on the curtain, mesmerised by the steadily falling flakes, which had already covered the tracks he'd made, settling in a thick layer on the garden and beginning to drift against the garage door. Then he walked upstairs to pull the curtains in the bedroom. It was only when he had finished doing so, at the window nearest the dressing table, that what was on it registered with him.

Her wedding ring, her engagement ring, and the Victorian garnet bracelet he'd bought her last birthday, ranged neatly together on the polished surface.

And in that moment he realised that since that incredible half-hour after breakfast, he had been existing in a sort of limbo, performing actions mechanically, shutting his mind off from what had actually happened. But that now he was going to have to face it and decide what to do about it.

At that moment, Nell Fennimore rang, and the lies began.

2

Time was, mused Detective Chief Inspector Mayo, when the Christmas holiday meant Christmas Day and Boxing Day and if either happened at the weekend, hard luck. Whereas nowadays, what with the New Year included, days in lieu, and it hardly being worth opening up for two or three days et cetera, et cetera, Christmas had become an indefinite extension. Never mind the crashing boredom that descended like a pall upon the nation, and anybody you needed being incommunicado for a fortnight.

This year, making matters worse, repeated falls of snow and freezing temperatures surpassing all records had further disrupted communications all over Britain, blocked roads, and several times brought motorway and city traffic to a standstill. In Lavenstock even the normally lively little Stockwell, cheerfully bubbling along to join the Avon, had frozen. Traffic Division, who were still having it rough, cursed the white Christmas and envied the rest of the strength with their lesser problems, confined mostly at the moment to minor incidents of a domestic nature—largely fights and squabbles due to too much alcohol and the unaccustomed and prolonged proximity of the nearest and dearest.

Mayo wasn't grumbling. Just before Christmas the worrying, several-months-old investigation into the disappearance of a young girl called Sharon Nicholson had been resolved. A depressing outcome, to an extent, in the sense that even though the girl had turned up safe and well, it had not been through police efforts. Sharon herself, who prior to her disappearance had shown no signs of emotional disturbance, had, it turned out, been finding her home pressures so intolerable she had eventually run away and been taken in by a conniving aunt. In the end, miserable and unhappy, wanting to go home but not knowing how, she'd preempted her own discovery by sending a Christmas card, easily traced by the postmark, to her mother.

The comparative lull after Christmas had given Mayo no choice but to plunge into the backlog of computer information about the enquiry which had avalanched on him and had to be dealt with in closing the case, and not least in finding answers to the sharp questions that were being asked. He thought it more than likely he might disappear and never be seen again under the weight of it. He was just easing the crick in his neck, in a moment of uncharacteristic depression, when the telephone rang in his upstairs office.

"Mayo here."

The voice of the woman police sergeant behind the desk came crisply, "There's a lady here would like a word with you, Chief Inspector, if it's convenient, a Mrs. Fennimore. She says you met last month when you gave a talk to her Women's Guild. Are you free, sir? She says it's important."

"Fennimore?" A vague recollection of a friendly person came back to Mayo. A further prod at his memory brought the realisation that she was the wife of the Fennimore who was the dentist up on Quarry Hill, a man with a successful practice and active in local affairs. He glanced at his watch. "All right, yes, I'll see her, Sergeant Jones. Send her up, will you—or no, tell her I'll be down in a minute."

"Right, sir."

"Thank you, Sergeant."

Mayo straightened his tie and ran a comb through the thick, short pelt of his dark hair: an ordinary man, with a serious, anonymous face which you wouldn't easily remember, except for the eyes, watchful and alert, and the sudden smile that totally changed his face. He smiled a little now as he shrugged his shoulders into a jacket that had seen better days. They hadn't been so formal the night before last, he and the sergeant, seeing the New Year in, raising their glasses in the uncarpeted sitting room of Alex's newly acquired flat that still smelled of the emulsion they'd put on over the weekend. A toast to the New Year, and perhaps to other things. Perhaps. Caution had become a key word in their still tenuous relationship, and not only for reasons of circumspection. Time will tell, thought Mayo, deliberately smothering his impatience and fondly imagining he was past the age to rush things.

Crisp as her voice, her dark hair a sleek cap, Alex Jones gave Mayo only a cool, blue-eyed professional glance and a general sort of smile as she introduced the woman waiting for him.

He remembered Nell Fennimore as soon as he saw her, a sensible-looking woman with dark curly hair touched with grey, warm brown eyes that were worried now as she asked if she could speak with him privately. She wasn't the sort, he decided, quickly summing her up, to waste time, her own or anyone else's; and he took her back up to his office, requesting some tea to be sent up.

Right away, she told him why she'd come, that she was worried about the inexplicable absence over Christmas of her friend, Fleur Saville. The story was so well put together, he knew she must have gone over it many times in her own mind previously; and, looking at her kind, sensible face, he guessed it had taken a good deal of soul-searching before she'd taken matters as far as this. He listened patiently to the run-down, about the preparations for the annual Christmas party given for disabled children by members of something called the Buttercup Club, on the Saturday before Christmas.

"We'd hired the church hall," she explained, "and spent most of the morning getting it ready for the party in the afternoon. Fleur had decided—that is, the committee had decided—not to have caterers, rather to get as many people as possible to contribute something in the way of food, so Fleur and myself and one or two others were very busy arranging the tables and so on as the stuff came in—and getting the games ready, of course. We worked until lunch-time . . . the last thing we said was that we'd be back at the hall at half past two. And that was it—Fleur just never turned up, and nobody's heard a word since. It's unbelievable! I know she wouldn't just go off like that, with never a word to me, or at least without some sort of explanation or apology—I'm closer to her than anyone. Except, of course, Edwin."

"Edwin being the husband?"

"That's right." She paused. "He has the bookshop down Butter Lane—antiquarian books, and maps, and things like that."

"I know it." Saville's specialisation in criminology had enticed

Mayo to step into the shop occasionally and treat himself to a book or two. Saville was a stiff, awkward man, he recalled, who seemed to have difficulty in smiling. "What has he to say about it?"

"He says there was a sudden crisis about the book she's writing . . . but you know, I'm afraid I do find that hard to believe. Fleur's just not like that. She's terrifically organised—you can't write twenty-nine books without being, *and* put in the time she does for charity, especially the Buttercup Club. She just wouldn't *let* herself have a crisis."

"A writer, is she? I don't think I know—"

Mrs. Fennimore cut in, with a kind of pride, "You'll have heard of her, though. She's Fleur Lamont." Mayo had, somewhere or other, but he was blowed if he could think where, until she prompted him by adding, "Historical novels."

He'd no difficulty then in placing her, seeing in his mind's eye the popular paperbacks with lurid covers portraying well-endowed females with revealing necklines. Not his sort of literature, but he'd have been hard put to it to count the times he'd come home in the small hours when his wife was still alive, to find her awake, reading, unable to put down the newest offering. Fleur Lamont had helped assuage more of his own personal guilt than he now cared to remember.

"Besides, to go off so suddenly, and leave Edwin on his own over Christmas, when he can't even boil an egg—it's just not on," Nell Fennimore insisted. "Especially not to the cottage, in this weather. It's not centrally heated, only a small open fire, and Fleur can't stand the cold. And I've rung and rung the cottage, and there's no reply."

"Lines are down all over the country. The snow's specially bad in Shropshire."

"I've checked—it's not a fault, there's just no reply."

"Could be, if she's busy writing, she may simply not be answering the phone."

In his own mind, Mayo hadn't many doubts as to what had happened. Fleur Saville had pushed off, almost certainly. Ten to one, with a lover. To spend Christmas with him—or the rest of her life. Something had sparked it off, a quarrel, or maybe the thought of spending the long holiday cooped up with that dry stick Saville had suddenly caused something to snap, and she'd simply walked out. People did it with monotonous regularity, walked out of lives that had, for one reason or another, become intolerable to them. Look at Sharon Nicholson. Only those closest to them couldn't accept that they left no traces because they didn't want to be found, and that in most cases they weren't. Nell Fennimore, for one, wasn't going to be satisfied with this explanation.

"You say her husband isn't worried?"

"He *says* not," she answered doubtfully, "but it's not easy to tell what Edwin's thinking or feeling. He's a very quiet man; he never says much."

Mayo could imagine that.

"Mrs. Fennimore," he said, choosing his words carefully, "I agree the circumstances of her going off so suddenly are unusual, and I understand how worried you must be. But I think you may have to accept the fact that Mrs. Saville might very well for some reason have left her husband. This so-called crisis about her book. Probably a bit of face-saving on his part, you know, until he can bring himself to admit it."

She said nothing for a moment, looking down into the dregs of her tea. "I realise that's the usual explanation, but you don't know them—how devoted they are to each other. He'd give her the top brick off the chimney if she wanted it . . . and she thinks the world of him."

How many marriages presented this devoted front to the world, and only when something like this happened was it seen to be a facade, a sham? He said quietly, "Then—what *are* you suggesting?"

There was another pause. Nell looked wretched. "I don't know," she said at last, faltering under his steady regard. "I really don't know. I just . . . well, have this feeling that something's terribly wrong."

"In an emergency, people don't always act rationally. If Mrs. Saville left in a hurry, everything else probably went out of her head; it didn't occur to her to let you know."

Nell clasped her handbag. "She wouldn't," she said stubbornly, "and another thing she certainly wouldn't forget, whatever the circumstances, was her inhaler."

"Inhaler?"

"Fleur's asthmatic, and she'd never so much as set foot out of the house without it—it's absolutely essential to her. On the morning of the party, she suddenly panicked, remembering she needed a new one. I offered to pick up her prescription at lunch-time as I was going into Boots anyway, and I've still got it, here." She took a small blue cylindrical atomiser from her bag and held it out to him.

"If she's so dependent on it, wouldn't she keep one in hand, not to run the risk of running out?"

"I think she usually did, but this time she couldn't have, could she? She reminded me several times not to forget; otherwise she'd be in trouble."

He sat, twisting the small tube round in his fingers, thinking. "Mrs. Fennimore, I'm sorry. There's not really anything to warrant starting an investigation at this stage, and I can only suggest you give it a few more days and see what turns up." He was being tactful. What he really meant was that he'd more to do with his time than chase runaway wives. "Meanwhile, though, I'll see if I can get someone from the local force out in Shropshire to check the cottage, make sure everything's all right." That wouldn't do any harm, and he was glad he'd made the suggestion when he saw worry and disappointment change to relief on Nell Fennimore's face.

"Would you? Oh, would you? I'd be so grateful. Probably I *am* worrying unnecessarily, but Fleur . . . she's more like a sister than just a friend, you see . . ." She hesitated. "Only, I wouldn't want Edwin to think . . ."

"We'll be tactful, Mrs. Fennimore."

She thanked him once more, seeming reassured at last by this big, solid man with his air of quiet authority, and stood up, preparing to go, then said awkwardly, flushing a little, "I thought you might possibly want to see a picture of her, so I've brought one with me." She opened her bag and handed him a photograph mounted inside a folder. "This is the four of us, taken at a Masonic evening earlier this year. That's my husband Gerald, there's Edwin—and that's Fleur."

Mayo recognised the bookdealer, his eyes fixed a little above the camera, looking uncomfortable in evening clothes, his tie slightly askew, unlike Gerald Fennimore, a very handsome man with dark wavy hair and something of a nineteen-thirties matinee idol about him, who wore them with panache. The focal point of the picture, however, although Nell too was in the foreground, was Fleur Saville.

He thought she would always dominate any group in which she found herself. There was something about her . . . not outstanding beauty, though she was very attractive and might possibly have had that quality some actresses possess, of making one think them beautiful. Small and slender, soft fair hair, winsome face, delicate and appealing, though there seemed to be an unknown quality about the closed smile. And it may or may not have been the shadow that made her chin seem a trifle overlong, the jaw a shade too firmly rounded. She was wearing a dress, dark and simply cut, that made Nell's bouncy pastel taffeta look schoolgirlish and unsuitable. He had the feeling she was the sort of woman of whom you might say, 'There's more to her than meets the eye.'

He handed the photograph back, but she said, "You can keep it if you want to."

She was indeed not going to give up easily, but he thanked her and put the photo in a drawer, then walked to the door and opened it for her. "If I hear anything, I'll let you know, Mrs. Fennimore," he promised.

3

"I'm not one to speak ill," Lola Tennyson announced over the washing-up, giving the chopping board a vigorous going over with Domestos and a hard scrubbing brush. "My religion's taught me that—but there's somethink up with them down Kelsey Road."

Nell wished she had the strength to say *her* religion forbade her to listen to gossip, but regrettably the mention of Kelsey Road immediately had her hooked, and after that, she really couldn't have borne not to hear. She compromised by saying nothing, rescuing one of her silver eggspoons that Lola was just about to attack with a pot-scourer.

"I mean," Lola went on, "my Debra went back to work yesterday after the holiday, and there was no instructions nor no typing nor nothink left for her. The study was all locked up, and he wouldn't open it—sent her home, he did. Not that it bothered her. She's a good girl—I'm not saying no different—but she can sit about all day, mooning—not like her mum, she isn't. Me, I just can't keep still," she added unnecessarily, as though the constant restless movement that drove everyone else mad was a trait to be envied and admired. "You ought to get your husband to buy you a dishwasher like Mrs. Saville's, why don't you? Everybody's got one nowadays."

Nell often asked herself whether Lola was worth the trouble, but the answer was yes, on the whole, and even if she hadn't been, kind-hearted Nell would probably have kept her on. Lola divided her time erratically between cleaning jobs for several different people, her skinny little figure zipping through her chores with speed —and attention, if supervised—permanently tuned in to the local radio station on the Walkman she carried around with her. She needed the money because she was, as she frequently reminded anyone who would listen, a one-parent family. Debra, who also worked for Fleur, had been a mistake. There were two other mistakes, besides. Emotionally feckless, her capacity for dashing about was equalled only by her capacity for getting herself into some kind of trouble: another disastrous love affair, non-payment of the H.P. on the latest expensive video, one of her offspring playing hookey from school. She remained unbowed, undaunted, she knew exactly what benefits she was entitled to under the Welfare State. Nell greeted Lola's twice-weekly arrival, and the next highly embroidered instalment of the serial story of her life, with a mixture of amusement, sympathy, and exasperation.

"She's got all the latest gadgets, hasn't she?" she went on, undeterred by Nell's silence. "He doesn't begrudge her nothing. Mind you . . ."

She gave Nell a sideways, encouraging glance, but you didn't gossip with Lola unless you wanted it told, with embellishments, all round Wrekin, and Nell decided she'd listened enough. She draped the tea-towel over the radiator, and said brightly, "Looks as though I'd better brave the weather and be off to Sainsbury's this morning—amazing, isn't it, all the food you stock up with over Christmas, how soon you've to start again?"

"Yes," Lola said, "mind you . . . what with that row they had just before Christmas, I'm not surprised she's decided to stop away for a bit and let things cool off."

"What was that you said?"

Lola nodded, her eyes gleaming like boiled sweets, relishing the effect of her bombshell. "That's right, Saturday before Christmas, at breakfast time, going at it hammer and tongs they was. I'd just got there; they must have forgotten I'd agreed to come in, just for an hour or so. I don't usually of a Saturday, as you know, but she needed a hand because of the party, see, for the kiddies, poor little mites."

"Quarrelling? Fleur and Edwin? Oh, surely not, Lola! You must have been mistaken!"

"Oh no, I wasn't. They wasn't bothering to lower their voices— and you could have knocked her down with a feather when she come into the kitchen and saw me, I can tell you."

"Well," Nell returned, with a briskness she certainly wasn't feeling, "everybody has their disagreements from time to time, I daresay. And it's not something they like to have talked about—is it?"

"Of course it isn't, but you know me, I'm not one to blab. If I hadn't been a Salvationist, I'd've been a Quaker."

The call from Shropshire had come in just before Cherry came into Mayo's office to speak about a call he'd had from Nell Fennimore.

The detective superintendent, spruce and well-brushed, hitched himself onto the corner of the desk, carefully adjusting the crease in his trouser leg, and listened to what Mayo had to say, not making any immediate comment. "Okay," he said finally, "I'm with you about not over-dramatising the situation; there could be a dozen reasons for what's happened—but for God's sake, don't let's tread on any toes over this. It might be best if somebody went and had a word, Gil." Mayo thought for a moment.

"I'll go myself."

"You? Oh. Well, you are already in on it, I suppose." The older man sounded apologetic, but relieved. It was a bit infra dig, not the sort of job he would normally have dreamed of expecting one of his senior officers to undertake, but perhaps, in the circumstances . . . tact and diplomacy . . .

"Better than Kite or anybody else putting their size tens in," Mayo said.

"Right. I'd much rather we didn't involve ourselves at all; we've had enough stick to take recently. But you know how it is."

Both men's eyes were drawn to the Sharon Nicholson files, inches thick, lying between them on Mayo's desk. The stick the superintendent was referring to went by various names—public accountability being the one bandied about at the moment, mostly in connection with the case of the missing girl. Stones had been thrown; the ripples went on widening. A few nights ago on television, the mother, who'd been so occupied with her own life she hadn't noticed her daughter was missing for twenty-four hours, had accused the police of not having done enough to find her, backed up now by the father, who hadn't seen either his wife or his daughter for two years. The sympathy of a large part of the public, who weren't aware of this, was with the parents. If the same public had ever experienced the grim atmosphere, the sleepless dedication of the men, fathers themselves, in any police station in the country when a child went missing, they might have spared some for the police.

Mayo understood Cherry's dilemma. Though differing in the degree to which they sought advancement, they were two of a kind: able, intelligent men, colleagues of some years' standing from the same part of the country, who took their jobs seriously and responsibly. In this instance, it was implicit between them that those concerned so far in this matter of Fleur Saville were people with clout, capable of making waves. Gerald Fennimore was a member of the Police Authority; his wife and Mrs. Saville headed more committees than Margaret Thatcher. They moved in circles that were important in Lavenstock—Rotary, Inner Wheel, and the rest . . . Mrs. Fennimore had already gone over Mayo's head in speaking to Cherry. The chief constable could be the next step.

The whole business was irritating and time-wasting, but the quarrel between Saville and his wife, reported by Nell Fennimore, did subtly change things, however reluctant the police might be to interfere in marital upsets. Cherry was right. They'd have to be seen going through the motions at any rate.

"He won't like it," Sergeant Kite said. "Police interference and all that." His expression was uncharacteristically sour this morning, he having spent most of the previous night with his long, lanky frame crouched behind a couple of noxious dustbins outside a Chinese takeaway, acting on a tip-off, waiting for a break-in that hadn't materialised until three o'clock. They'd nabbed the villains okay, but by the time everything had been wound up, it hadn't been worth going home, so he'd stayed in the office to write up his report, fortified by a couple of bacon butties and a pint of strong coffee.

"We can't win anyway, lad. We'll be accused of sitting on our backsides if we sit tight and do nowt and summat *has* happened to her."

The sergeant looked speculatively at Mayo. This deliberately assumed Yorkshire persona of the D.C.I. was always more evident when he was keeping something up his sleeve—or when he was about to pounce. Kite wondered which it was now.

They'd worked together for long enough now to have got each other's measure. Mayo knew that his sergeant's sometimes flippant manner, his inclination to jump too fast to facile conclusions concealed a shrewd intelligence and a willingness and capacity for hard work that he liked. He was keen and took a pride in his work. On the other hand, Kite was learning that you had to be patient where Mayo was concerned; he'd tell you what he wanted, when he wanted. As when you made what you thought was a brilliant deduction, and more often than not found he'd been there hours before. This apart, Kite considered he could be suffering worse fates than acting as fall-guy for a man like Mayo, who didn't stand on ceremony and didn't bite your head off all the time, as long as you went easy on the 'sirs.' All in all, Kite acknowledged, the D.C.I. wasn't so bad.

"I'll walk across and see Saville myself now; my back's broad enough," Mayo announced. "Get a bit of exercise besides." Never given to explaining himself overmuch, he said nothing about his talk with Cherry.

Kite, who'd expected to be sent himself, and hoped to be told to send D.C. Farrar, was relieved at not having to miss his hot lunch, but surprised, as well he might be. "Not coming over to the Saracen's, then?"

Mayo patted his waistband. "Three and a half pounds surplus to requirements on the bathroom scales this morning, Martin." His daughter Julie, studying at catering college, had made sure he didn't go hungry over Christmas.

He didn't explain, as he might have done, the true reason for skipping lunch. Mayo, essentially a practical policeman, had found one of the drawbacks to promotion was that unless you made damn sure otherwise, you spent more time sitting at a desk and less and less time where it mattered. Besides, he was beginning to get that tingle, that faint prickle of intuition, that there might be something about the Saville case that wasn't quite as it appeared.

The shop in Butter Lane was, as he'd half-expected, closed. Most of the smaller shops in Lavenstock still kept to half-day closing, and Saville hadn't struck him as the sort to defy tradition, so he decided to continue his therapeutic walk down Church Walk and along by the public school playing fields, across to Kelsey Road, to see if Saville was at home.

Most of the pavements in the town had now been cleared for easy walking, though in the suburbs and across the river on the hilly slopes and in the narrow streets, amongst the small, grimy factories and engineering shops of the old industrial part, it still lay in the dingy, inconvenient heaps where it had been shovelled, overlaid with soot. Only out in the villages, Brome and Seton End and Grendon, was it still white, hard-packed, and deep-frozen. After eleven days, some of the country lanes were still impassable, even yet. Mayo thought suddenly that there might be a slight, a very slight, softening in the air, a dampness. Or was that wishful thinking, due to a definite feeling of having had enough of this lot by now, old-fashioned white Christmas and all?

It had been a good holiday, though, the best since Lynne had died. Maybe because, one way and another, Alex had spent quite a bit of it with them. Alex had always been a favourite with Julie, and her stock had gone up several more points more since the time she had helped so admirably and unobtrusively during Lynne's last illness. Newly independent herself, Julie had no qualms about speaking her mind. "Why don't you two get married, Dad?" she kept asking.

"Why don't you stop matchmaking, love, and get on with your cooking!"

If only it were as simple as that.

When Alex had had herself transferred to his division, shortly after his own transfer here, a new beginning after Lynne's death, he had speculated as to why, tentatively reaching a few conclusions of his own. For one thing, he didn't altogether believe that she'd come here solely to be near her sister, who'd opened the fashionable interior design business on the corner of Butter Lane. For another, she'd never married, and here *he* was, now free and unattached, still young enough . . . not all that old, anyway, not much the wrong side of forty. They got on well together. It seemed to stack.

That had been some time ago. They'd progressed since then. But the more you saw of Alex, the more you realised what you couldn't take for granted. And that was the third thing. Mayo wasn't an optimist. He'd early cottoned on that when everything seemed to be going for you, when things were just right, as like as not that was the moment when life chose to turn round and kick you in the teeth.

He gave a small grunt and turned into Kelsey Road.

It was a pleasantly mixed sort of road, houses of different styles and sizes which had grown up haphazardly since the mid-nineteenth century. Number twelve had been unpretentious but well built when put up in the nineteen-thirties, and had now settled into a graceful and prosperous middle age with its matured garden, creeper-covered walls, and a market value over a hundred percent higher than its original cost.

Edwin Saville showed Mayo into a front sitting room that faced the road, with a longish strip of garden between, at present hidden under billows of soot-specked snow, pitted with the tiny arrows of bird footprints. The drive didn't appear to have been cleared of snow since the first fall; it lay hard-packed under the car-tracks which led to the garage.

Saville did himself well, Mayo thought. It was a roomy house, without being too big, comfortably if conventionally furnished and decorated in colours that painstakingly "picked out" the colours of the chair covers. There were some good pictures and a few choice pieces of well-waxed antique furniture, and besides the warmth from central heating, a huge fire burned in a York stone fireplace. Books filled shelves on either side, the gold lettering on their spines glinting in the firelight.

Saville looked taller and thinner than Mayo remembered, and he had a fearful cold. He was wearing a shapeless old pullover of the nondescript drab-green called "lovat" over grey Terylene trousers of an old-fashioned, baggy cut, and Rupert Bear slippers, the sort of clothes an eighty-year-old pensioner might have worn. Waving Mayo to a seat on the sofa, he walked across to where, on a table beside a hide-covered wing chair, stood a cut-glass whisky decanter, a jug of water, and a tumbler, together with an old book, leather-bound and with thick, fuzzy-edged pages. He blew his nose and held up the decanter. "Drink, Inspector?"

"I won't, thanks, not at the moment."

"No? Oh, of course not."

A short silence fell between them, while Mayo decided where to begin. When he'd introduced himself at the door, Saville had invited him in without asking his business, and made no attempt even now to do so, a thing practically unheard of in Mayo's experience. Most people couldn't wait to know what you were after them for. The impression Saville had made on Mayo at the times he'd been in Saville's shop was stronger than ever, an impression either of extreme reserve or complete disinterest—or maybe, thought Mayo, feeling charitable, that feverish cold was just about as much as he could cope with.

There was nothing to indicate the lack of a woman's presence in the house. Everything was neat and dusted, and a large bowl of blue hyacinths on a nearby table, giving off an overpowering scent that reminded Mayo of funeral parlours, was only one of a number of bowls of other flowering plants. But there was the cleaning woman to do the chores, the Mrs. Tennyson who'd overheard the quarrel. He cleared his throat. "I understand your wife's away from home, sir?"

"Yes, that's so." At last there was some reaction, even if it was only a slight wariness in the way Saville raised his head.

"We've been making enquiries on behalf of a friend of hers, Mrs. Fennimore—"

"*Nell?*"

"That's right. She's been trying to contact your wife, but couldn't get hold of her, so she asked our help. We've had no luck either—"

"Why should Nell do that?" Saville interrupted, now evidently quite nettled. "Why get on to you? She'd no right. I told her Fleur was at the cottage."

"It was only that she began to get a bit worried, what with the weather and the cottage being so isolated and all that. I'm sure you can help us sort it out, make sure your wife's all right, sir."

"She was perfectly all right when I last spoke to her."

"When would that be?"

"Oh, I forget, a couple of days ago. I haven't been bothering her every five minutes . . . she went away for some peace and quiet, after all."

"She's been at the cottage some time, I believe? Since before Christmas?"

"What are you getting at, Inspector?" Saville's voice had suddenly sharpened. "My wife happens to be a busy writer. Her American publishers have been pressing her for sight of the book she's currently working on, and she decided to take herself off and work on it until it was finished. That's all there is to it."

"Over Christmas? Must have been miserable for you, sir."

"Christmas doesn't mean anything to me."

"No, it's not the same as it used to be when we were lads, is it?" In the interests of drawing people out, friendliness never hurt, and Mayo had no hesitation in aligning himself in age with Saville, in disregarding the probable ten years and more difference between them. "Too commercialised by half. Still. It was the twenty-second she decided to go, the Saturday?"

Saville nodded, taking refuge in another bout of sneezing, so that his expression was hidden.

Mayo waited until it was over before continuing, quietly, "What would you say, Mr. Saville, if I told you they had snow in Shropshire a day before we had it here—and much worse? That the lane to your cottage has been completely blocked since the twenty-first of December, the day before your wife left . . . and still is?"

The feverish colour left Saville's cheeks with alarming rapidity, leaving behind a greyish pallor, and the atmosphere in the room became uncannily still, charged like the minutes before an electric storm. Suddenly he reached out and splashed a quantity of whisky into his glass, and drank. It went down without touching the sides and brought two spots of hectic colour back to his cheekbones.

"Oh, my God." He sat slumped in his chair, desolation limning his face.

"I think you'd better explain, sir, don't you?" Saville appeared not to hear. "Mr. Saville?" Mayo said, more sharply.

"She's not at the cottage," the other man said at last. "Never has been, as far as I know. She's—the truth is, she's left me." This evidently distressing admission was brought out in a rush, harshly and with so much difficulty that after the effort he seemed incapable of further speech, but there were questions still to be asked and answered.

"I'm sorry about that, sir, and I realise this must be very upsetting for you, but I take it the reason she left was because of the argument you had earlier in the day?"

Saville stared at him and then smiled, or very nearly. It was the first time Mayo had seen even the faintest trace of amusement cross his face, and in the circumstances it was painful to watch, almost grotesque, like a man smiling in the face of a death sentence; it vanished as suddenly as it had appeared. Nevertheless the brief flash revealed a different man and with it, astonishingly, the ghost of a hidden charm. Without further expression, Saville remarked, "Lola Tennyson, I presume?"

"It was brought to our attention that she'd overheard you quarrelling, yes. Perhaps you'd like to tell me about it?"

They never quarrelled, he and Fleur, never. He because he rarely cared sufficiently to make an issue of anything; Fleur because somehow in the end she'd always get her own way, anyway, with that sweet gentle persistence of hers turning the situation to her advantage, or if that failed, simply going ahead. And usually, he didn't mind very much.

This time he *had* cared, and Fleur had known he would never give in . . .

In October, he'd been persuaded into taking an off-season holiday and going with her on a cruise to the Greek islands, a happening Edwin had hoped to forget as quickly and completely as possible, and never, ever to repeat. Not that it hadn't been memorable, in its way; they'd seen the Acropolis by moonlight and walked in the footsteps of the gods, but the company—and the food! He hadn't had a decent, simple English meal for a fortnight. So that he'd been as astounded as ever he'd been in his life when Fleur, that Saturday morning, over breakfast, put forward her proposal, all cut-and-dried and thought out, for them to buy a place on one of the islands, sell up and go there, to live, permanently. It wasn't as if they'd be without friends; there was quite a colony of expatriates on many of the islands, she'd gone on, gently persuasive. Of course, it would mean Edwin giving up the encumbrance of the bookshop, and taking early retirement. But that didn't matter; there'd be no need for him to work, because of course she could carry on with her writing just as easily there as here. Think of the saving in taxes alone.

She'd never before objected to paying taxes; she earned more than enough—and the idea of "retiring" at all was ridiculous to Edwin, at whatever age. His father had died at a book auction, at the age of seventy-six, and Edwin could think of no better way to go himself. As for the bookshop being an encumbrance! He almost panicked. His life, his love, his refuge, gone. But no, the whole idea was so ludicrous, it had to be one of those outrageous fantasies of hers, which even she didn't really believe in. He couldn't credit she was serious.

She was, though.

But so was he. Not even the emotional blackmail of how much better it would be for her asthma could persuade him to give in.

It was a deadlock, and it resulted in the only quarrel they had ever had in their married lives, and because it was unique, it was monumental.

Only later did he begin to wonder why, why she had even contemplated for one moment going to live—to *live!*—in that place, unspeakable in summer and consisting no doubt in winter of a blank half-life in a half-climate, neither one thing nor the other, thrown together, willy-nilly, with other aliens. He shuddered with horror at the mere thought, then remembered the handlebar-moustached, bridge-playing, gin-drinking Waterton, a fellow passenger on the cruise, from whom he'd always escaped faster than politeness would allow. Fleur had laughed, saying dear Bunny was at least amusing and knew how to treat a lady. He could dance, which Edwin couldn't; she was always in his company; they forever had their heads together; he'd told her of his plans to go out there and live . . . Edwin's realisations, like his regrets, came too late.

Mayo let Saville run on, spilling out his story compulsively. He wasn't sure he could have stopped him. He let him continue until at last his voice trailed away; he leaned back and closed his eyes, looking physically, as well as mentally, spent with the effort.

"Well, sir, that's a lot different from the story you put about in the first place, isn't it?"

"At first, when I found she'd gone, I told myself she must be at the cottage, that she'd decided to stay there, just for a while, you know—to get over the row we'd had."

"Did you try to get in touch with her there?"

"Yes, I did. When there was no answer, that was when I knew I'd been fooling myself. I knew she must have gone to that—fellow."

"Forgive me, but wasn't that assuming rather a lot? A shipboard acquaintance of only a couple of weeks?"

"You think so?" Saville's mouth twisted. "Well, I've never been much of a catch for her. I'm twelve years older than she is, and I'm not up to the sort of life she was apparently envisaging—though I never pretended I was." He stared into the fire in a silence that stretched out drearily into the empty years ahead, a man who knew his own inadequacies, but could be no other. Poor devil, Mayo thought. "But I was sure at least she'd come back to collect her work. It means so much to her, she'd be bound to come back for it; and then I could persuade her to stay, and nobody need know she'd ever left. Well," he ended harshly, "she isn't going to, is she? She's never going to come back."

"Oh, I don't know. A bit final, that, after just one quarrel, surely? You can't be certain she won't ever return. Freedom often looks different from the other side of the fence. Or did she," Mayo asked, with sudden suspicion, "leave you a letter telling you what she intended to do?"

But Saville looked astounded, as though it was utterly incomprehensible that his wife should write to him. "No, she left no letter."

"And of course you've checked to see how many of her clothes have gone?"

The question was met with the same blank look. "I'm not sure I'd know, anyway. I don't notice these things."

"Passport? No? Money from the bank?" Another shake of the head. Mayo sighed deeply. "Well, what about her car?"

"She didn't drive." That was a surprise. Most women of Fleur Saville's status not only drove, but possessed their own car. "She wasn't mechanically minded. And when I wasn't available, there was always someone else willing to ferry her around."

"All the same, I suggest you check up on those things."

Saville regarded him somberly. "I can imagine the way your mind's running. You're thinking something terrible might have happened to her?"

Mayo said cautiously, "It's always on the cards, I'm afraid."

"You can count it out in this case. She went of her own accord, entirely. She has no intention of coming back."

"You sound very sure."

"Oh, I am, I am. Because she left behind her wedding ring and her engagement ring. Even the bracelet I bought her. Right there on the dressing table, arranged in a row. You can't be more final than that."

Mayo almost bit his tongue in an effort not to say what he would have liked to say. If Saville had told him this in the first place, he could have been on his way twenty minutes ago. Fleur Saville had, after all, in the manner of many another bored or disillusioned wife, simply run away. It had happened just as he, Mayo, had thought it had.

All the same, he was struck by Saville's manner, which seemed to him curiously ambivalent, making him wonder what *would* happen were Fleur Saville suddenly to return. Would Saville be prepared to forgive her? Mayo was oddly certain that he would not— there would be no going back in Saville's book—that he was a man with the utmost fixity of opinion, for whom there was nothing as dead as a relationship he regarded as finished.

He left the house in a very thoughtful frame of mind.

4

The thaw began slowly at first, with a barely perceptible rise in temperature, then came more swiftly when the rain began in earnest overnight. The next morning, when the hard-frozen snow had melted just sufficiently in the lane, where bluebells would grow in spring and the beeches would be a glory in the autumn, the body was found.

The lane had no name, being little more than a track, only just wide enough for a car, deeply rutted, and with rough thickets of brambles on either side. It formed the long side of a triangle of land lying in the angle of a crossroads that quartered wooded heathland, outstandingly beautiful at most other times of the year.

The woman had a name. She was Fleur Saville.

She'd been there some time. Since the Saturday before Christmas, in fact.

"We might be a bit off the beaten track, but that doesn't mean it's not busy out here," said Ken Anstruther, the unfortunate young man who lived in the small, isolated cottage centred in the triangle of land, and who'd found the body. Not only found, but recognised it. He was badly shaken, and was talking to reassure himself. "That crossroad's a bloody menace—people use *that* road to bypass the Birmingham road, and *that* one from Seton End into Lavenstock. They all go too fast."

Several police cars were parked just inside the entrance to the lane, which debouched onto a sharp curve of the main road, a hundred yards from the crossroads' awkwardly angled intersection. A blue revolving light on the patrol car first summoned to the scene flickered on the faces of dripping, rain-caped men moving about in the half light of early morning, beginning to rope off the area around the body.

"Are you suggesting it might be a hit-and-run, sir?" Kite asked.

"Well, it could be, couldn't it? The visibility's bad here, to say the least, and folks tend to get impatient, waiting to cross. That's why we ourselves in normal circumstances always use the back entrance from the cottage into the lane here to avoid the crossroads —saves getting held up. You can wait forever there."

There was an edge of grievance in his tone. In another moment he'd be bringing up speed limits and roundabouts. "It's a fairish way from the main road," Kite pointed out, "where she was found."

"Perhaps she crawled here after being hit, or someone picked her up and carried her—how should I know?"

Mayo joined them in time to put an end to these hypothetical theories. "No point in jumping to conclusions before we hear what the doctor has to say; he'll be here any minute."

A hit-and-run accident in any case would be established by the nature and position of bruises to the body, he thought, making his own speculations. But what, in that case, had Fleur Saville been doing out here—going for a walk in the middle of December, miles from anywhere? In sleet and snow? In those shoes? *And* without her handbag. In his experience, women rarely went anywhere without a bag of some sort.

The rain pelted onto the treacherous surface of the lane, and Mayo almost lost his footing as he turned to speak to Anstruther. "Perhaps we could go inside and take your statement, sir, while we're waiting for the doctor." Anstruther had found the body, and whether he liked it or not, he was an important witness, even though he was innocent. If he was innocent.

"Yes, come on. I'll make some coffee," Anstruther said abruptly. "Real coffee."

Kite prepared to go with him with alacrity, looking as though he didn't care what kind of coffee it was, as long as it was hot, a sentiment with which Mayo entirely agreed. The mobile police canteen should have been here by now. Where the hell was it? Theoretically, the weather must be warmer than it had been of late, since a thaw had begun, but it felt cold enough to freeze brass monkeys.

He paused briefly beside the body before following the other two, and stood looking down at it once more with the stoic expression of one who has been forced to accept the frequent sight of unnatural death, but still has no stomach for it. It was a grim experience for anyone—though considering it was a two-week-old corpse, this one was less sickening than most. Subzero temperatures had seen to that, preserving it and arresting decay; that and a two-foot layer of deep-frozen snow which had protected it from the rats and crows. Apart from its now sodden state, the body looked much as it would have done shortly after death—the only visible injury a deeply lacerated contusion on the left temple. She lay abandoned, face upturned to the lowering sky, fair hair dark with rain, a layer of snow still under her. Beneath the red coat she was wearing a straight black skirt and cashmere sweater, with a many-stranded pearl-and-gilt necklace, fine black tights, and elegant high-heeled black patent shoes. He stared hard at the hands, small and ringless, with short, unvarnished nails, and thought of the photograph he'd seen of her, taken at that dance, the poignant contrast between it and the stillness and finality of her present state. He felt angry at the waste. There was little doubt in his mind that this was murder. He could smell evil. But these were private thoughts and personal intuitions which had better be kept to himself for the time being. It hadn't after all simply been another case of a woman leaving home, as he'd been convinced. Fleur Saville must already have been dead for eleven days when Nell Fennimore first came to see him.

"I reckon that's about it." D.C. Napier began to pack up his photographic equipment, with the air of one not being sorry to do so.

"Then cover her up," Mayo said abruptly, hunching his shoulders into the turned-up collar of his raincoat. "And get a grip on yourself, lad," he added to the very young uniformed constable next to him, who was looking distinctly green about the gills. "You'll see worse than that before you've done."

"Yes, sir."

Leaving the mackintosh-caped and booted figures to get on with their thankless task of searching, as best they could, for any least thing that might be of significance, Mayo followed his sergeant. He was glad for the young constable's sake to see the mobile canteen turning into the lane as he did so. He remembered what it was like.

In Edwardian times the cottage had been some sort of shooting lodge on the Seton estate, a one-storey building that careful restoration and the addition of a small garden had made as charming as a toy cottage on a model railway layout. It was neat as a new pin, outside and in, a self-contained little place with a white picket fence matching the scalloped trim to the roof, small conifers and beds of winter-flowering heathers poking through the snow around the porch entrance, and more pot plants than Mayo had ever seen together in anyone's house placed in artistically arranged groups in the large through living room. Noticing was part of his make-up, as well as his official training; he stood beside an eight-foot monstera while his quick, comprehensive glance took in the general *ambiance* of tan leather, fashionably rag-rolled walls, and understated comfort.

"People don't realise that one can practically furnish a place with pot plants," Anstruther remarked, pleased to observe the interest of the two policeman as his neat, compact figure emerged through the jungle with a steaming pot of coffee and a bottle of Rémy Martin, with which he proceeded to lace their coffee, using a lavish hand. "If only they did! We'd be a great deal richer."

"We? Just yourself and your wife live here, sir?"

"I'm not married," Anstruther replied shortly. Mayo eyed him briefly. "Myself and my partner. He shares the cottage with me— and the business." The other man's name he gave as David Garbett, and the business they shared as the Broadfield Garden Centre, just this side of Lavenstock.

"And you say you used the lane this morning for the first time since before Christmas, sir?"

"That's right. The last time was the same Saturday evening it began snowing; we were bidden to a so-called party, which I have to tell you was horrendous. One of those awful business thrashes with weak punch and warm white wine, and all the smoked salmon gone by the time we got there. The snow gave us a good excuse to escape early, but even so, by the time we reached home, the lane was impassable and we had to drive in by the main gate. It always drifts along there, nothing to stop it, really. It comes, as they will insist on saying, straight from Siberia."

"You left home at six, and you're sure the body wasn't in the lane then?"

"We'd have been bound to notice if it had been. You saw for yourself how little room there is—and we were going very carefully. It was already a bit dicey, so much so that we debated at the time whether to stay at home or not, but in the end we decided the main roads would be clear enough."

"What time did you get back?"

"Let's see—there was a re-run of *The Godfather* on at nine, and we were just in time to catch the beginning, so—"

So, judging by the depth of snow which had covered her, and the relatively small amount underneath her, Fleur Saville had probably lain there since just after six. Kite noted the place where the party had been held and the times, and asked, "What about this morning?"

"We usually leave together, David and I, but today he had to pick up some cut flowers from the wholesale market in Birmingham, so he left half an hour earlier. He used the front entrance since he was going in the opposite direction."

"Then you were alone when you came out the back way, at around eight?"

"Eight precisely, when I shut the door," corrected Anstruther, who was evidently a very precise person, "plus two or three minutes more to get the car out."

"The lane's been undisturbed since the snow fell?"

"Totally, I swear. Virgin snow, until the thaw. In fact, it was a mistake to try to get out that way this morning. I should have waited." He poured himself more coffee, added another splash of brandy. His hand was not altogether steady. "It was her red coat I saw first . . . then her face . . . my God, it was a shock, I can tell you."

"I'm sure it was," Mayo said, "especially as you knew her."

"Well, I didn't *know* her, not in that sense. I just knew who she was. I got out to have a look; I thought something had blown into the lane, and when I saw her face, I thought, Christ, I've seen her before—it's that woman who buys all those flowers, that Mrs. Saville."

Mayo recalled the scent of hyacinths, the bowls of cyclamen that had filled the Savilles' sitting room. "You only knew her as a customer?"

"That's all. But you don't forget someone like her—she spent more money with us every week than most people spend in six months."

"And you'd never met her socially?"

"I've told you, no. That's the only time I ever saw her, when she came into the centre. Here, just a minute, what are you getting at?" He gave a short, angry laugh. "My God, I only *found* the body; I didn't damn well kill her!"

"No-one's suggesting that, sir. Merely a matter of routine questions, that's all," Mayo answered, neutrally official. "But it's important we have a full signed statement from you. If it's convenient, I'd like you to accompany one of my officers down to the station now to make it."

Anstruther opened his mouth, but one glance at Mayo's face evidently told him he'd be wiser to make sure it was convenient. He'd misread the expression, however. Mayo was thinking that Anstruther's involvement in the case was probably just what he said, and no more. He seemed truthful, and the eyes, he thought, were honest. It was just his misfortune that he'd found the body.

"She's been missing since the twenty-second of December," he told the doctor, stamping his feet. The rain had stopped, but the cold had not. "Two weeks, and this lane's been blocked since then. That squares?"

"More than likely. Impossible to be precise under these conditions."

Never bloomin' well hang himself, Ison wouldn't, Mayo thought as the other man straightened up, easing the crick in his neck and taking his glasses off to rub his eyes. He'd come straight from the scene of a multiple motorway pile-up caused by the abominable road conditions, and being up half the night had done nothing to improve his temper. His eyes were bloodshot, his face unshaven. He peered out from the fur-lined hood of a parka, his breath making a cloud on the air. Scott of the Antarctic wasn't in it, poor sod.

"How? How did she die?"

"I'm only here to certify she's dead, not to pass opinions at this stage."

"Come *on!*"

Ison grunted. "Well, no apparent sexual interference at any rate. I'd say either her head struck some sharp object, or some sharp object struck her head." He added irritably as Mayo made a sound of impatience, "I'm not joking. You'll have to wait for Timpson-Ludgate's P.M. before we can say for certain, but if she was hit, the injuries to the brain will be at the point of impact. On the other hand, if her head struck a stationary object, a stone or something . . . Speak of the devil."

The purr of a twenty-year-old Rover, polished and maintained in a state of pristine newness, heralded the arrival of the pathologist, Timpson-Ludgate himself, rotund, bouncy, and cheerfully energetic, looking as though he'd just had a bath and a good breakfast. His pride in his motor was equalled only by the relish with which he undertook his daily examination and dissection of corpses that had arrived at their ends by various violent or unnatural means.

"Morning, morning, what have we here?" Broadly smiling, he approached the group assembled round the body and bent to view it with a metaphorical rubbing of hands, but as the polythene sheet was removed, a startled exclamation escaped him, "Ye gods, you know who this is?"

Mayo said that she hadn't yet been formally identified, but they had reason to believe she was a Mrs. Saville.

"It's Fleur Saville, all right. Ye gods," he repeated, affronted, "she's a friend of m'wife's!" As if she'd committed some unforgivable breach of good taste, being found dead in such circumstances. It was the first time Mayo had ever seen the pathologist put out at the sight of a corpse.

He left the two doctors to their consultation and walked thoughtfully back along the lane. The track emerging through the snow was grass-grown, worn through to soft sand in two parallel tracks made by the few vehicles which used it. Stones against which the victim might have fallen and fatally banged her head were in such short supply as to be virtually non-existent. The possibility of accident was, in Mayo's mind, remote.

"But in any case, somebody else was involved," he said aloud. "It's not on a bus route, she didn't drive, so somebody brought her, or put her here. Why *here?*"

One of the group of officers he was addressing coughed. Detective Constable Deeley, a big, beefy lad. "Good-tempered, slow. Works well under supervision," had been his last assessment. "Is beginning to think for himself," Mayo might now have added. "I know this lane pretty well, sir. Nobody uses it much now, except courting couples—" One of the constables at the back of the group sniggered, and Deeley stopped, reddening as he realised what he'd said, looking sideways at Kite, but Kite wasn't in his usual mickey-taking mood that morning, and let it pass. "I mean—"

Mayo said impatiently, "I know what you mean. I haven't lost my memory." Which wasn't what Deeley had meant. "Get on with it."

"Well, so maybe somebody intended to dump her body in the old gravel pits, but found the lane was blocked and had to leave here where she was found."

"Gravel pits?"

"That's where the lane lands up, eventually. They're supposed to be very deep, and they've been abandoned for yonks, sir."

Mayo decided he'd go along and have a look himself, but it was very likely the explanation for the body being found here. He gave Deeley a congratulatory nod. "Well done, lad." The young D.C.

blushed furiously above the Lord Kitchener moustache that was his pride and joy.

"So what next?" Kite asked.

"So treat it as foul play until we know otherwise," Mayo said.

5

Lavenstock wasn't renowned for its beauty, but it had its moments, especially on days when the sun shone on the river or touched the tall spire of St. Nicholas's church and the Tudor brick of Lavenstock College, the minor public school that gave a touch of class to the town. Moreover, since the bypass had arrived and a shopping precinct had been created, new vistas had opened up, revealing once more the pleasant jumble of old lanes, courtyards, and buildings where Lower High Street and Sheep Street sloped down to the river from the Cornmarket. Mayo's liking for the busy little market town was growing in proportion to his increasing knowledge of it. It was beginning to have the familiar air of a shabby old friend, easy to live with mostly, sometimes exasperating, but tolerable even today, seen through the murk of the disagreeably heavy, damp mist which had succeeded the rain.

Butter Lane was one of the more venerable of its old alleyways, some of its buildings dating back to Tudor times. It had been slowly going to the dogs for years. The shops were small, inconvenient, uninteresting, and out of the way. But with the soaring rents of premises in the newer part, the lane had lately been rediscovered, and many of its ratty old buildings were suddenly experiencing a renaissance. The fashionable "Lois Fielding, Interiors" on the corner, the one belonging to Alex's sister, had been one of the first. Now the lane boasted—whitewashed, black-beamed, and restored—a small, hopeful dealer in antiques, a shop devoted to selling lace, a health-food store, a home bakery, and Saville's bookshop. Here the refurbishing had stopped.

Peering through the dusty bow windows of the narrow building and into the musty interior, with its low ceiling, rows of dim volumes, and faded maps, it was just possible to discern an old-fashioned mahogany counter, with a pair of library steps no-one could have made the mistake were there to persuade customers to linger. There appeared as usual to be no sign of life within.

Mayo stood with his hand on the door, bracing himself to face the always harrowing task of having to tell someone that a relative had been found dead, possibly murdered, even when, as in this case, the relative was likely to be the chief suspect. He had never yet found a way of doing this easily. He reminded himself sharply that his own finer feelings were not in question: it was his job to be interested in Saville's reactions.

"Come on, let's get it over with." He squared his shoulders and pushed open the door.

Zoe was with him, in the back of the shop, when the bell rang.

Zoe, her pale face sharp and taut under the thick, shining copper hair that burned like a flame round her head. Comfortable old sagging chairs drawn up to the powerful gas fire. Used coffee cups and the remnants of the teacakes she had brought in from next door and toasted before the bars of the fire . . .

Edwin knew how it would look through the eyes of the two policemen as he showed them into the back: shrewd men who weren't easily deceived by anything, who must have picked up the vibrations of shared laughter and intimacy that had been there a moment or two ago, killed abruptly by the interruption of their own unwanted presence.

Zoe had already jumped up, prepared to go, sending a swift, intuitive glance from one to the other of the two men. She knew they were policemen before he told her.

"Please stay, Zoe."

He saw with relief and gratitude that she recognised this immediately for what it was, a plea rather than the polite formality it sounded to be. Hesitating, she threw a brief enquiring glance at the chief inspector, and on receiving a confirmatory nod, re-seated herself.

"If I might just have your name, please?" Mayo asked her.

"Henderson." Edwin waited stoically, questions and emotion suspended, hearing her quick, assured voice that held its own familiar ironic emphasis as she added, "Mrs. Henderson. I live across the way from Mr. Saville, just off Kelsey Road."

They wouldn't understand about his friendship with Zoe. Who would? He wasn't sure he understood it too well himself. Except that he could talk to her with an ease he'd never experienced with anyone else. He admired the wry way she looked at life, and she could make him laugh with a genuine deep amusement which not many people—not even Fleur, with all her vaunted sense of humour—often managed. Like a bright, clean flame she illuminated the darker corners of his life.

Sex hadn't yet entered into the equation as far as he was concerned, partly because the difference in their ages was enough to scare him off with its overtones of a father-daughter relationship, but mainly because Edwin, married to one woman, was not the sort to entertain, however briefly, thoughts of going to bed with another.

"Don't take life so seriously," she'd said to him within an hour of their first meeting. Which had been a new thought to Edwin, a naturally serious, introverted man. He was still trying, several years later, to act upon the advice.

A slight cough roused him. He blinked, came back, and at the chief inspector's next words knew that his deepest fears were to be confirmed: the horror which he'd hidden, refused to acknowledge even to himself, was about to manifest itself.

"Mr. Saville, I'm afraid I have some serious news for you . . ."

The next few minutes rushed over him like water over someone who was drowning, but some of its meaning must have penetrated the roaring in his ears. He understood that they had found her. They were asking him to go with them to identify what they called "the body"—good God, they meant Fleur!—they talked of a post-mortem, and of taking a detailed statement of his movements on the day she vanished. The implications of that had scarcely made their impact before the next words struck him like a blow . . . they would need to "take a look around" his house.

It was gone, over, the privacy he had always so jealously guarded. His personal life would once more be open for all the world to view . . . the quiet, bookish routine of his days, which was all he ever asked for, would again be disturbed and disrupted.

Saville had taken it quietly, too quietly for Mayo's liking, staring down at his feet, withdrawn into himself, letting Mayo speak without interruption. Only when he eventually raised his eyes was the torment evident, and even then Mayo wasn't sure what it was about. Nor even later when, his gaunt features a mask revealing nothing, and what little colour he'd had having fled his face, the man stood looking down at the dead body of his wife.

They left him waiting in the interview room at last, in the charge of D.C. Farrar, while Mayo and his sergeant went to grab a sandwich and some tea. "Couple of hours like that, God, that's what earns you your salary," Kite remarked, straightening the tie he'd loosened as they walked down the corridor, whose overheated air felt fresh in contrast to the room they'd left. Saville seemed to use up all the air around him. His negative approach had a deadening effect. But keeping to the book, holding on to your patience and your temper, being persistent without using bullying tactics . . . in the end they had a statement from him, which was presently being typed out. Not that it amounted to much. He was sticking stubbornly to the story he'd given Mayo when he'd originally spoken to him at his home.

"So, Mr. Saville, let's go back to the beginning, starting with why you lied in the first place—all right, then, deliberately made misleading statements—about the reasons for your wife's disappearance. Why you said she'd gone to the cottage to finish her book."

"I've already explained. I thought she'd gone away to get over the disagreement we'd had—and I couldn't think of anywhere else she'd be likely to go."

"In weather like that? How did you suppose she'd have got there? She couldn't drive, you said."

"She'd have hired a car with a driver. She did, when she went to the cottage alone."

"Something she often did?"

"Not often. Sometimes."

"But then, when you knew that story wouldn't hold water, you told a different one entirely, didn't you, that she'd left you for another man? Mr. Saville, are you quite sure there isn't yet another version?"

When a suspect began to change tack, it was the first sign that he was cracking, that he might give if you leant on him. But Saville, though sweating a bit, had clearly decided the point had come when he wasn't going to be moved from the stance he'd taken.

"What I've told you is what I believed to be the truth. After the argument at breakfast, I left for business. When I came home and found she wasn't there, I knew it meant she'd taken the quarrel seriously. The cottage was where she always went when she wanted to think things over, with regard to her work, and I reckoned that's where she'd gone this time. Then I found her jewellery sitting on the dressing table."

He stopped, and Mayo deliberately let the silence continue, until at last Saville, a rising note of desperation discernible in his voice, broke it. "You must see what it looked like to me! Leaving the things I'd given her there like that, after we'd quarrelled! Her wedding ring, her engagement ring. As if that summed up everything she felt about me and our life together—that hurt, I can tell you. Not even troubling to leave a note."

He slumped against the back of the hard, straight chair after this barren conclusion, running his hand over his brow where the sweat had gathered, his shoulders hunched. Mayo felt the uncomfortable sense of voyeurism he often felt when witnesses, at their lowest ebb, revealed to him things they probably had never admitted even to themselves before, but he was accustomed to not liking himself very much over what he often had to do—and anyway, in Saville's last few words, he recalled, there had been more than a touch of remembered anger overlaying the evident hurt; what had started out as justification had become an accusation.

"You actually believed she'd gone for good, simply on the strength of one quarrel?"

"Yes, I did. It was typical of Fleur to make some fancy gesture like that. But what I believed was no business of anyone else's, not even Nell's. If I chose not to tell the world she'd left me, that was up to me." Saville shut his mouth stubbornly and sat heavy and passive, possibly regretting having said as much as he had, while Mayo watched him. Mayo didn't say anything either.

His first impression of Saville had been of a naturally secretive, private man, that explanations or excuses for his actions would never be given freely, would indeed have to be dragged from him, and nothing he'd heard during the last hours had given him cause to change his opinions. That uncharacteristic outburst might well be—would almost certainly be—the last. He let it go, knowing he could come back to it later.

"All right then, we'll leave that for the time being."

He nodded to Kite, and together they began to take Saville once more in detail over the fatal Saturday.

"Tell me again, when was the last time you saw your wife?"

"At breakfast," Saville repeated, with a weary sigh.

"You're sure of that?"

"Of course I'm sure."

It seemed that he was accustomed to spending the greater part of his working days alone, often without speaking to a soul apart from his wife, at lunch-times, when he shut the shop at one for an hour and a half and went home. Not the lunch-time of the day she disappeared, however. That day, above all, he had chosen not to go home. Mayo asked him why. Not hungry, Saville shrugged, but when pressed, he admitted that the quarrel he'd had with his wife had upset him too much.

"I'd told her I wouldn't be home. I was being rather cowardly, I suppose. Afraid the difference of opinion we'd had might start up again, that I might even be persuaded to give in to that outrageous idea of hers of selling up, going abroad, simply to put an end to the whole thing. I dislike arguments; it's so much easier as a rule to avoid them, and in the end, what does it matter? There are very few things ultimately so important that they're worth generating a fuss about."

He'd said much the same sort of thing before, and a dark and dangerous philosophy it was, it seemed to Mayo, this kind of accidie. Taken to its extremes, one that could generate an indifference towards the importance of anything—even the value of a human life.

"But you've told me this was more than a 'difference of opinion'; in fact, it mattered a lot to you?"

"Yes, it did. And that was precisely why I thought we both ought to have the opportunity to cool off, until we could talk the matter over rationally."

It sounded reasonable enough. Mayo wasn't sure he believed it. "So where did you have your lunch?"

"I shut the shop up as usual at one, made myself a cup of coffee, which was all I wanted, and stayed in the back until I opened again at half past two."

"Did you leave the premises at all during that time?"

"No. That's what I've told you. I stayed there."

"Alone the whole time?"

There was perhaps the faintest hesitation. "Not if you count the woman who keeps the bakery next door. She came knocking on my back door to ask if she could park her car in my yard." Disapproval drew down the corners of Saville's mouth. "She's always doing it; she knows I can't very well refuse. There's never much room for parking down Butter Lane, but my yard's often free because I walk to the shop, unless I need to use the car for some reason or other."

"What time was that?" Saville shrugged.

"Possibly just before two-thirty, I don't remember. I'd no reason to keep looking at my watch."

"And what time did you finally shut up shop?"

"I closed early, at four-thirty. I had some books I wanted to take home to look at."

"Closed at half past four?" Kite put in. "And went home to *read?* On one of the busiest shopping days of the year?"

Saville said remotely, "There's not much call for old books in Lavenstock at any time."

Especially his sort. If he'd read a tenth of his stock, he must be an expert on murder in all its ramifications, Mayo thought, reflecting that this opened up interesting avenues of speculation into other facets of Saville's character, and even possibly into aspects of the murder itself. "Tell me, how do you manage to keep your business going if there's as little trade as that?"

"I get by. Much of my business is done by post. I advertise monthly in the literary press, and I do have my regular clients, collectors with specialist requirements and so on."

"You had *some* customers in the course of the afternoon, presumably?" Kite asked.

"One of my regulars came in, just to browse around—Mr. Howe, the headmaster at the Comprehensive; he's often in on Saturdays. And a woman who came in to pick up a map she'd bought and left to be framed. Her name doesn't immediately come to mind, but it'll be in my order book. They were the only two customers I had, but at what times, I couldn't say. Early on, I think. Oh, and about half past three I suppose it would be, Mrs. Henderson popped in."

Mrs. Henderson. Zoe. A mass of flaming hair in a fashionable uncombed tangle, a brightness about her. An enigmatic face, nevertheless. About twenty years younger than Saville, at a guess.

Mayo could tell, even before the next question came from Kite, that he'd evidently been thinking pretty much the same thing. "Why? What was she there for?"

"Does there have to be a reason for a friend calling in? As a matter of fact, she brought in a frame she'd been repairing for me. She's an expert restorer; that's how she makes her living."

"How long did she stay?"

"I didn't time her. Long enough for a cup of tea and a chat."

"Fifteen minutes?"

"Possibly."

"I see. Anyone else?"

"No. I saw no-one else all afternoon. Apart from Mrs. Tennyson on my way home—the person who helps my wife in the house." Saville explained his brief encounter with Lola on her collecting round.

"And after you got home?" Mayo asked.

"I had something to eat, then fell asleep in front of the fire. I saw and spoke to no-one all evening."

"Except, of course, for speaking to Mrs. Fennimore on the telephone."

"As you say, except for her."

They were back to square one. Mayo sat for a while, chin on his hand, watching Saville, but at last, sensing the interview had gone as far as it profitably could at this point, he stood up to indicate it was at an end. "That's all for the moment, Mr. Saville, unless my sergeant has anything—?" He raised an eyebrow at Kite, but after a glance at the hieroglyphics he called notes, Kite shook his head. "We shall need to see you again, of course, but all we want now is for you to sign your statement; then you can go home."

"Like you said, he can't make all that much of a living, selling those old books—yet it doesn't seem to have left him on the breadline, does it?" Kite remarked. "House in Kelsey Road, and all."

"In this case, probably earned by the sweat of his wife's own fair brow."

"Oh, well, yes."

Kite seemed to think that a matter of luck, as if he couldn't envisage writing being *work*, which, considering Fleur Lamont's highly successful career, was unlikely, but he added thoughtfully, "It'll be interesting to see how much she's left—and who to. My guess is Saville."

"Sure—but first things first. Which is to trace her last movements. You get along to Mrs. Fennimore this afternoon; she could be able to give you a list of the helpers at that children's party. They were the people last known to have seen her, and one of them may give us some sort of a lead. Then there's this Waterton and any possible relationship with him to be established—we'll keep an open mind about that, though I'm inclined to think Saville may have blown it up. You'll have your hands full, Martin, and I've a meeting with Cherry over this Sharon Nicholson thing sometime this afternoon, but later on I'd like to get down to Kelsey Road. I'm not sure we're likely to find anything there after all this time; it'll probably be a waste of time, but it'll have to be done. As I'll be down there, I'll fit in an interview with Mrs. Henderson."

He's enjoying this, Kite thought, pushing back his chair and preparing to carry out his orders. All right for some, no wife and kids to go home to! He thought of what he'd planned for his family over the next couple of days, and cursed inwardly. Yet another lousy weekend up the spout! Incautiously, he said as much.

"If you can't stand the heat, get out of the kitchen." Still sorting out the priorities of the enquiry, Mayo spoke idly, only half-thinking as he did so.

"Hell, it's not that!" Kite answered, stung.

Mayo threw a quick look at his sergeant. "What's up, Martin?"

"Oh, nothing." Kite was regretting that he'd spoken, remembering also that Mayo had mentioned tickets (in the plural . . . Kite had noticed, and speculated) for that concert at the Town Hall in Brum tonight—which he wouldn't now get to. Kite hoped whoever the second ticket was for would understand. A woman? Once or twice ideas had occurred to Kite, linking Mayo and Alex Jones, but nothing definite. Both of them were adept at playing their cards close to their chests—and a very nice chest it was, in Sergeant Jones's case. Kite wouldn't think the worse of Mayo for that. But whatever the D.C.I. had had on his mind for weeks now, it hadn't brought a smile to his face. He'd looked tired and strained, acted irritably.

Kite knew, from sources other than Mayo himself, because Mayo's private life was very much his own, that his dead wife had sometimes given him a hard time over his job, and who could blame her? Not many women could take his sort of dedication—and it wasn't easy, whichever way you looked at it, being a plain clothes copper's wife. Twice as hard if there were kids and the wife had a career, as in his own case. They had their moments occasionally, he and Sheila, over the extent of his commitment to his job, the amount of time he could devote to his family; of course they did, but it wasn't serious, though it had made him think, from time to time. Martin Kite, though not an overly sensitive or deep-thinking man, was very far from being a fool. He was ambitious and sufficiently clued up to realise that frustrating himself by giving up the only job he'd ever wanted to do in all his life wasn't going to be much help to his wife and family in the long run, either. Sheila, bless her, understood.

His attention caught by the sharpness of Kite's tone, Mayo's mind was brought back to his own lost weekend. Damn, he'd forgotten that! Well, it couldn't be helped, he'd just have to hope Alex wouldn't be too put out, though she'd been looking forward to the Brahms concert, he knew. He'd have to be a bit more tactful with her than he'd been with Kite. He realised he'd unintentionally got his sergeant on the raw with his unthinking remark and tried to repair the damage. "Sorry, lad, I know how you feel," he apologised, "but there ain't much we can do about it."

"That's okay." Mayo was relieved to see that Kite hadn't taken offence, but his was a buoyant nature, never down for long. "Anyway, with a bit of luck we'll have this lot all sewn up by Monday," a hopeful assumption that earned him a sardonic look from Mayo.

"We shall, shall we?"

"Why not, it's pretty open and shut, isn't it? I have this feeling Saville's having us on. He was obviously lying. He *must* have gone home at lunch-time. It'd take less than ten minutes each way. They met there and the row continued where it had left off, ending with him killing her."

Mayo wasn't yet prepared to commit himself as far as Kite, nor waste time on theorising before they had more evidence. He had his own reservations about Saville, in that he wasn't as sure as Kite appeared to be that he was lying, merely that he was keeping something back, but he had to admit that was the most likely thing to have happened. And how blessedly simple it would be if so. Another investigation like the last he could do without just now. Anyhow, it was something to work on, for a start. They weren't about to go looking for complications at this stage.

"Maybe it wasn't deliberate," Kite was going on, "maybe he just pushed her and she fell, hitting her head. He wouldn't be the first husband that's happened to. Panics when he sees she's dead, decides to get rid of her body. Goes back to the shop to establish some sort of alibi, and as soon as it's dark, shuts up and comes home, takes her rings off to give credence to the story of her having left him, and then drives the body up to Seton End, intending to throw it in the gravel pits."

"Then why wait till six o'clock? It was dark enough well before five, and the snow was getting worse all the time. And why leave her there in the lane when he couldn't get through? There was nothing to stop him taking her back home until he'd either thought of another way to dispose of her, or until the snow had gone sufficiently for the lane to be passable. He wasn't to know it was going to last as long as it did. And there's always the possibility that Saville had hit on the truth," he said. "That she had intended to leave him. That she met her lover somewhere, and *he* killed her. Waterton, maybe—Bernard Waterton, wasn't it?"

"Company director of a small-builders' merchants. Known as Bunny—but he looks like a dead duck. We telephoned him, but his housekeeper told us he's been on a safari holiday in Africa since the beginning of December."

"Check that. Though it could just as easily have been someone else."

"Or," said Kite, "the boot may have been on the other foot. It may have been Saville who had someone else in mind. And I don't think we've far to look, have we?"

Mayo thought about Zoe Henderson, her enigmatic face. She'd said nothing more that morning after giving her name and address, until Saville had been told of his wife's death, when she had jumped up and taken hold of both his hands, murmuring something which only Saville could hear. He hadn't replied, but all the same, Mayo had the impression that he had been comforted.

"No, we mustn't forget Mrs. Henderson," he said.

6

Mayo's driver pulled up in Kelsey Road behind the Scenes of Crime van and a row of other police vehicles, parked as near the kerb as the banked snow would allow, inviting the attentions of a small group of loiterers, hopeful of some excitement. The team which had been awaiting his arrival emerged from their van as his car drew up. Other men were already busy making house-to-house enquiries down the road on the off chance that someone might remember seeing something out of the ordinary as far back as two weeks ago, with Christmas intervening, and, who knew, they might be lucky.

"No need for you to hang about as well; I'll find my own way back," Mayo instructed his driver, as he got out of the car and was joined by the other officers.

"Right, sir."

A uniformed constable began moving the reluctant bystanders on as the group of detectives walked towards the house. Mayo led the way, shouldering his way past two men and a young woman, sprung apparently from nowhere when they spotted him, waving the three of them and their notebooks away with a brief promise of more information when it was available—his usual policy of keeping the press happy with as much truth as he could reveal, so that they didn't need to invent too much.

Saville had been allowed to go home some time earlier, and it was he who opened the door to Mayo, his hands cradled round a steaming mug of soup, looking hunted. "Oh, it's you. I thought it was another of those reporters."

"Been bothering you, have they?"

"They have their job to do, I suppose."

"Take my advice and say nothing to them—they've already been given a statement," Mayo told him, realising with grim amusement even as he did so how superfluous his advice was. They'd be lucky to get anything out of this one. When Mayo asked permission to go over the house, an indifferent shrug indicating he might go where he pleased was all the answer he received.

On his previous visit Mayo had seen only the flower-filled and book-lined sitting room, and glimpsed a formal dining room through the open door from the hall, itself dark-oak-panelled in the mock-Tudor style favoured at the time the house had been built. Now he had time to register the thick Persian-type carpeting that ran from the front door and up the stairs, the well-polished antique chest, and the collection of framed embroideries and samplers on the walls, and to notice a small, inconspicuous door which, when he opened it, he found led to the garage with Saville's three-year-old blue Granada estate reposing in it. He closed the door, and as he turned back into the hall, found Saville's watchful eyes upon him. The man shrugged again and drifted into the sitting room, while Mayo went upstairs, leaving the downstairs search to be conducted as he'd directed.

In his experience, most people's lifestyle reflected their earnings, tending to over- rather than underreach. He was well aware that writers on the whole earned far less than people generally imagined; Fleur Lamont, however, had been in the top-selling class, but it wasn't reflected in the way the Savilles lived. They didn't go without anything, that was for sure, but neither could they be said to live in the lap of ostentatious luxury.

He threw a comprehensive glance around the restrained ivory and gold of her bedroom as he entered. Indubitably hers, though shared with Edwin to the extent of twin beds and his own wardrobe. An expanse of pale carpet, ivory-painted furniture, touches of gold and cut-glass on the dressing table and turquoise silk curtains. One wall of mirror-faced cupboards. Entirely feminine, with nothing of Saville's personality at all stamped on the room.

Mayo moved carefully and methodically around, opening cupboards and drawers with hands enclosed in plastic gloves, taking time to make his own assessment. Surprisingly few clothes hung in the wardrobe, though most of them bore the kind of labels which showed they weren't bought in High Street stores. Dress bows were stuffed with tissue paper; each pair of Italian shoes had its set of trees; silk underclothes lay neatly folded on shelves. Her handbags were empty, with everything no doubt carefully transferred to the one the change of outfit demanded.

He stood thoughtfully, for quite a while, before moving on to the dressing table, where her make-up drawer was just as immaculate, with not so much as a crumpled tissue or a few hairs left in either comb or hairbrush. How many of us, he wondered, could suddenly depart this life leaving such impeccable order behind? It was unnatural.

She didn't die here, in this house, he thought suddenly. He didn't know what made him so sure. There's been more than time to get rid of anything incriminating, and he hadn't exactly expected to find bloodstains on the carpet. But the certainty was there.

Edwin Saville's possessions, unlike his wife's, were untidily kept, not to say scruffy. His shoes were put away without being cleaned—they'd have to be taken away for examination and the mud on them compared with the mud in the lane, as would his clothes, which were mostly of the well-worn, leather-patches-on-elbows kind. Two of the drawers in the chest by his bed were devoted to clean linen, immaculately laundered, but the top one was filled with assorted junk—long-forgotten keys, pencil stubs, old diaries, an empty spectacle case, several defunct batteries, cough lozenges, not a little fluff. Mayo was reminded of a small boy's pockets.

There was nothing more that need interest him upstairs. Besides the main bedroom with its connecting bathroom, three other bedrooms and a second bathroom led off a spacious upper landing, two of which were guest rooms decorated with Laura Ashley co-ordinated fabrics and wallpapers, their drawers and cupboards empty, and the third a box-room, seemingly undisturbed for some time.

He went downstairs and through the dark-panelled hall again, with its dining room on the right.

"Find anything yet?" But they seemed to have had as little success as he himself.

He could see Saville through the open door of the sitting room, standing with his hands in his pockets staring through the window, with the lost-dog air of someone feeling like a stranger in his own home. He looked rotten, still in the throes of his cold, turning round listlessly as Mayo went into the room. "Have you finished?" he asked dully.

"Not yet," Mayo answered briefly. "Where did your wife work, sir?"

"Work?" Saville repeated, as though he'd never heard the word. "Why, here, at home." Mayo suppressed his irritation and spoke patiently.

"Which room did she use as her study?"

"Oh, I'm sorry, I thought . . . sorry, through here."

He led the way through the hall and then through a recently modernised kitchen, designed to look as though it were in some idealised country farmhouse, with hanging copperware and strange gadgets dangling from butchers' hooks. A strong ersatz smell of the canned oxtail soup Saville had been drinking pervaded the air, but everything in here, as everywhere else throughout the house, was almost aggressively clean. Mayo was beginning to think the forensic team might as well go home. He wasn't giving much for the chances of finding anything at all in this house in the way of evidence.

"Out there." Saville was pointing through the window to a building of timber construction, about the size of a double garage, which Mayo had seen from upstairs and thought perhaps was some sort of workshop. "We had it put up specially, two or three years ago. You'll need the keys. It's always kept locked—hasn't been opened since she . . ." Leaving the sentence unfinished, Saville brushed a hand across his forehead, then brought a bunch of keys from his pocket, from which he selected one, preparing to lead the way.

"I'll find my own way, thank you."

The building reminded Mayo of Doc Ison's surgery, without the waiting room. It was divided into two, the front half being a small office equipped with the usual filing cabinets, desk, and an electronic typewriter—no word processor, he noticed.

The larger half was obviously the place where Fleur Saville had worked, he surmised as he entered it. This too was workmanlike, close-carpeted in brown haircord, with plain cream walls, two of which had bookshelves floor to ceiling. Several of the shelves were devoted to copies of the novels of Fleur Lamont in various English and foreign editions. There were two comfortable-looking office-type chairs and no typewriter. One of the chairs was drawn up to a plain, sturdy oak table, which she'd evidently used for writing, since the delicate little secretaire standing in front of the window, though one of the prettiest pieces of furniture Mayo had ever encountered, would have been practically useless for any real work. He walked across to take a closer look at it.

It was made of some golden wood he'd an idea was satinwood, gilded with ormolu, inlaid with marquetry, the different-coloured woods worked into extravagant floral designs on the top and the drawer-fronts. He thought it might possibly be French, over-ornate for his personal taste, but its quality couldn't be denied, even to a confessed amateur such as he. It struck an incongruous and frivolous note in this unadorned room, he thought, squinting across the highly polished surface. And what d'you know? Clear impressions of fingerprints all over it. He retraced his steps, called for Dexter.

"Here a minute, Dave." He took the detective constable back with him to the study. "Get the prints off that, will you, I want to go through it. And when you've done, there's a car in the garage you'd better begin on till I give you word you can come back in here."

Leaving Dexter to his insufflators and camel hair brushes and aluminum powders, Mayo occupied himself with an examination of the contents of the drawers and cupboards in the other room, putting aside the business correspondence and files relating to the various charities with which the dead woman had been concerned. When the main study was free again, he went back and unlocked the drawers of the secretaire with the tiny ornate brass key on the ring Saville had given him.

The drawers were as immaculately neat as he expected, with

every paper in order. This seemed to be where she'd kept her personal papers, and he spent some time flipping through her chequebook stubs, credit card flimsies, bank passbooks and statements. He also came across her passport.

It appeared that Fleur Saville had paid the bills for the running of the house and almost every other incidental expense that occurred, including insurances, the cruise to the Greek islands they'd taken in October, repairs to Saville's car. Apart from her expensive clothes and the amounts she'd spent on flowers, they'd apparently lived well within their means, within the very healthy income accounted for by her considerable earnings. He'd suspected she must have earned a tidy sum, but the actual amount made him raise his eyebrows. There was no copy of her will.

Making a mental note to ask Saville for the name of her solicitor, Mayo walked across to the window and stood looking out over the long, narrow garden, bounded by a beech hedge, its leaves warmly golden brown against the snow. Beyond lay Lavenstock College playing fields, then the rosy red-brick grouping of the school buildings themselves, a quiet and agreeable outlook for a house so near the town centre, though today the buildings loomed through the darkening afternoon, and the normally clear, melodious strike of the ancient clock on the chapel tower, leisurely giving out the hour across the fields, sounded muffled. By the wicket gate at the bottom of the garden, a fat corgi rushed aimlessly about, yapping, while its owner, patiently waiting, stamped his feet, shot his cuff to check his watch with the clock, and yawned.

"Isn't that a lane running between the bottom of your garden and the school tennis courts?" Mayo asked Saville when he had retraced his own soggy footprints through the snow and back to the house, carrying the files and papers he wanted to take.

Saville replied that it was a track of sorts, but that it led nowhere, except back to the main road. "It's a bit of no-man's-land; nobody uses it much except as a short cut to the park. Or sometimes it's useful if you want something delivered to the back of the garden."

"There's access for vehicles, then?"

"With difficulty, and only when it's dry. It's too full of potholes otherwise. You could easily get bogged down."

It hadn't been dry on the twenty-second, and there'd been several days' rain previous to that. Any car trying to park there in such conditions would run the risk of getting stuck, at least of being noticed. All the houses had long back gardens, and neighbours, from their upstairs windows, would have a long view.

He said to Saville, "I haven't come across your wife's jewellery—the things you found on her dressing table. I'd like to borrow them if I may. You'll be given a receipt for them—and for these." Saville regarded the stack of files expressionlessly.

"I'll get them for you."

He was gone only a few minutes, returning and opening his fist to drop the jewellery into the plastic bag Mayo held open. Insofar as could be seen at a glance, the bracelet appeared to be a pretty example of Victoriana, a double row of garnets set in marcasite. Her wedding ring was a broad gold band, the engagement ring also gold, a conventional twist of two diamonds and a central ruby. Nothing remarkable, considering what events they might have set in train.

"Police investigations have begun into the death of Fleur Lamont, the well-known historical romance writer whose body was found early this morning buried in a deep drift of melting snow near the village of Seton End, and who disappeared from her home in Lavenstock on December 22, the Saturday before Christmas. The police are not ruling out the possibility of foul play. Miss Lamont . . ."

She snapped off the radio, which had been tuned in to the local station, and whirled round, white-faced. "Did you hear that? You'll have to tell them now, Mick, you'll just have to!"

"Not on your nelly! Come on to bed—let's have an early night."

"Listen, won't you, somebody's bound to have seen you going in and out; it'll look so *bad* if you leave them to find out."

She was little and dark and fierce, and he loved her more than he had ever loved any human being, even his mother, but not even Jane was going to make him go to the police.

"What about your fingerprints?" she went on. "You didn't wear gloves or anything, did you?"

"Why should I have done? Jesus, I was only taking what's mine by rights! Anyway, they'll have been dusted off by now. If I know dear Fleur, the sort of cleaning woman she'd employ wouldn't dare leave so much as a tea leaf in the sink."

But panic screwed up his guts as he remembered his hands running all over the desk. His mother's desk. And fury scalded him again when he thought of *her* using it—one of the very few things she hadn't chucked out, as if all memory of his mother must be obliterated, as though she'd never existed. He'd stood in front of it, stroking the golden inlaid satinwood, remembering his mother telling him how it had belonged to her great-grandmother, who'd been given it by a French countess who was said to have received it —and it may even have been true—from Marie Antoinette, but anyway it was the most precious thing they had in the house. He'd tried all the drawers and found them locked. He couldn't have forced the locks without damaging the desk, and he'd been tempted to take it, contents and all. Except that eventually having to touch *her* papers—possibly even parts of the current tripe she was writing—would have made him throw up.

"Mick, don't ruin everything, being so stupid! When we've got so much going for us, at last." Jane twisted the brand-new, shiny wedding ring, and he saw her eyes dart round the doll's-house room, cosy and warm, furnished on a shoe-string and now enhanced with the small treasures he'd "rescued" from Kelsey Road: the slightly foxed Victorian water-colours, the little nursing chair that only needed re-covering, the framed family photographs, and the bow-fronted mahogany chest of drawers.

"And what'll happen if I do go, hmm? And they find they've already got my dabs? D'you reckon they're going to say all right, now go home and be a good boy? With my record? No way!"

"You'll never learn, will you?" In desperation, she banged her small fists against the table. "I've no cause to love the fuzz, God knows—I haven't yet forgotten the demos they've dragged me from by my armpits—but they're not fools. You've nothing to be afraid of. You're innocent!"

Not as innocent as you, darling Janey, not by a long, long way, for all your Cambridge degree and your clever ideas and advanced opinions.

"Mick" she said. *"Mick?"* And her lively, intelligent eyes as she looked at him grew wide and dark with fear.

7

After leaving Saville's house, Mayo crossed the road to the opposite side, the as yet ungentrified, less "desirable" side, in the house agents' parlance. But house agents were not, in his experience, renowned for their sensitivity, and the appeal of Zoe Henderson's house was elusive. It lay in a tiny, surprising cul-de-sac, end on to Kelsey Road, the last of a stepped terrace of three small, unremarkable artisan-type houses which some enterprising builder at the turn of the century had taken the opportunity to squeeze into a space left between the gardens of larger ones on either side. Large, funereal conifers dipped sweeping branches over their high, old walls to enclose the little street in a witch-like darkness where the one dim street lamp threw grotesque and slightly sinister shadows. The lowering skies of the day had brought an early dusk, moisture-laden. The thaw dripped slow and heavy.

She wasn't expecting him, but she showed no surprise, opening the front door and standing back to let him enter, drying her hands on a towel. He was invited to step straight from the darkness outside into a long, knocked-through room, vibrant with colour, furnished for comfort and use with the careless skill of someone very certain of their own taste. It had great style. He was aware of what he vaguely thought was Arts and Crafts period furniture in square, strong oak, and William Morris-style wallpaper. A pierced Gothic-type screen painted in medieval colours stood in one corner, some plain elegant silver with insets of coloured stones was displayed on a table. The coal fire burning in a black iron grate threw leaping shadows onto shining, polished flagstones graced with richly coloured rugs. He spoke with spontaneous admiration.

"I like your house, Mrs. Henderson."

"Do you?" She regarded him coolly, through beautifully shaped eyes, their colour the light, greenish-blue of aquamarines, slightly tilted like those of a cat. "My husband hated it. I rather fancy it myself." She smiled faintly, showing small, pointed teeth. "Will you come through? I've something on the boil that I can't leave."

He followed her, past a circular dining table covered in floor-length red plush, through to the back, expecting, knowing the lay-out of such houses, to find himself in the kitchen, and indeed one end of the room they entered made concessions in the way of a stove and a sink, cupboards, and a small pine table. But most of the available space in this glassed-in extension was her work-room, cluttered by the paraphernalia of her trade. Saville had said she earned her living as a restorer—of anything, it seemed, from china to furniture, and Mayo looked with interest at the pieces scattered around in various stages of renovation: a chest stripped to the bare wood, an iron-framed Victorian armchair ready for reupholstery, an elaborate picture frame with part of its moulding missing. The place was pervaded by a smell of glues and solvents, polishes and paints, and whatever it was simmering on the gas burner. He hoped the latter wasn't food.

"Sorry about the smell," she said, divining his thoughts and plugging in the electric kettle before spooning instant coffee into mugs. "I'm used to it, but if it puts you off we can go into the other room, only I'd rather like to finish this thing first."

"What is it you're doing?" He accepted coffee from her, which she made without allowing the water to become quite hot enough.

She bent to the surface of the small wooden chest she was work-ing on, her head bright under the focused beam of an anglepoise lamp. "Making this look old. It's called antiquing if you try to sell it as a copy, faking if you pass it off as the real thing. I assure you I don't do that—pass it off, I mean, though some of my efforts have fooled quite a few people." She broke off to look up and give him an ironic, faintly mocking smile, and then became totally absorbed once more as she dipped a ridgy old paintbrush into some kind of dark varnish and drew it quickly and expertly over the lid of the chest, then, using a rag, blurred it in.

Her hands were small, with thin, strong fingers that moved surely. With another small brush, she retouched the carving and moulding round the edges. The chest was already beginning to look used, worn with time. He glanced from it to her absorbed profile, the beam of the lamp lighting the taut planes of her face. Good bones, her nose small and very straight, a narrow-lipped mouth curved up at the corners, firm chin. She moved slightly and her profile became half-obscured by the curtain of rich hair. A woman like this might easily dazzle a man like Saville. What might it be like, he wondered, with a sharp, unbidden stir, to feel the warmth of that vibrant hair through one's hands? She carefully put aside her brushes, and as she looked up, their eyes met.

"I was thinking, I have an old bracket clock," he said, "that has a small part of the veneer missing on the case. Could you do anything with it?"

"I'd have to see it before I could tell you." He knew that she knew damn well what he'd been thinking, and that it hadn't been anything to do with clocks; there was a gleam in those slanted eyes that without doubt showed secret amusement. "Why don't you bring it along and let me see?"

"I'll do that, when I've a bit of time." Or maybe he wouldn't.

"Good. Well, now that stage's finished, I'll clean myself up and we can talk properly. I can come back to it later; that's one of the joys of living alone."

"Your husband?" he asked as she washed her hands at the sink and then came back to where he was perched on a stool, and picked up her mug. "The one who hated your house?" The way she'd first mentioned his name, and now this further oblique reference—Mayo knew that it wasn't forbidden territory, that the question had possibly been invited.

"It wasn't really the house he hated; it was my obsession with it. He couldn't compete, so he threw in the towel. God, this coffee's horrible; I can't think why mine's always so much worse than other people's. Let's chuck it away and go and sit somewhere comfortable and have a real drink."

He could see the husband's point of view. He handed over his undrunk coffee without reluctance. When she'd discarded the fisherman's smock she'd been working in, he saw that she wore the same flowing garments as yesterday, a full, longish printed skirt, flat-heeled Russian boots. With her pale face, the undisciplined hair, he fancied she saw herself as part of the furnishings, as a Rossetti girl, a latter-day Janey Morris perhaps, whom she resembled slightly.

Back in the glowing sitting room, she switched on lamps, drew the curtains, stirred the fire, threw on some more coal and poured Martini. When Mayo saw how she mixed it, more gin than vermouth, he was glad he had declined. "I learned the proper way to mix a martini in America, where they sometimes *spray* on the vermouth," she offered, seeing his attention on the way she'd fixed it. She raised her glass and took a sip, watching him over its rim; then she leaned back, the smile fading, staring deep into the fire.

He waited; time was passing, but he felt it wouldn't be good tactics to rush her. Besides, he felt reluctant to move. Despite her terrible coffee and, judging by her kitchen, her probable disinterest in all forms of cooking, she had, he thought, aware of his own tiredness, the gift of making islands of comfort and intimacy. Like now, like the cosy scene in the back of Saville's shop yesterday.

"It's all a mess, isn't it?" she said at last, in a low voice. "Horrible and somehow—degrading. But I suppose you're used to it—murder, I mean. It was murder, wasn't it?"

"We're treating it as such," he said carefully, interested in her use of adjectives, "and we never get used to it, Mrs. Henderson."

"I'm sorry, I didn't mean—"

"I know what you meant." He hadn't intended to sound pompous. "How well did you know her?"

"Fleur? Not as well as I know Edwin."

He waited. It was Edwin he wanted to know about as well.

She shrugged, and said carefully, "We often go together to the same sales—I have a small van, but it's old and only about fifty percent reliable—and he's able to put quite a bit of work in my way, one way and another. For instance, I do all his framing. Edwin's one of those people who grow on you, you know. He takes a bit of getting to know, but he's worth it when you do, an interesting man, and extremely kind and—gentle, under that reserve. *She* never saw that—but it's true. So if you're thinking he killed her, you'd much better look for someone else. And that's all there is to it."

Oh, there was much more to it than that, he'd swear—just how much he'd have given a lot to know. He had a very strong feeling that there were undercurrents between the Savilles and Zoe Henderson which had not yet been revealed. "Tell me about Mrs. Saville—what she was like?"

"I don't think," she answered, her mouth twisting in a funny kind of way, "that I should be an entirely unprejudiced witness."

"Why is that?" On surer ground now, familiar territory, his own country of interrogation and answer, he watched her steadily whilst still speculating on the nature of the friendship between her and Edwin Saville. An ill-assorted pair, but he had seen stranger affinities.

"Since you ask, I didn't like her much. She was clever, and beneath that soft, sweet manner she manipulated people for her own ends."

"That's not the picture we have so far."

"That's what I mean. She was clever enough for it not to be apparent that it was their emotions she was playing on, or for them not to care. They were dazzled by her glamour, and she had this sweet reasonableness—charm, I suppose—she had folks eating out of her hand . . . Edwin most of all. People were always saying how talented, how creative she was, how kind—they couldn't see the other side of the coin. Only they'd better not get tired of buttering her up. There were times when she could be a not very nice lady."

Her chin was raised in a sort of defiance, but when she reached for her glass he saw that her hand was trembling slightly. "See what I mean—you'd much better not take notice of me; I'm talking off the top of my head. Or maybe out of the bottom of a glass." She raised her drink, but the level of the martini had gone down hardly at all.

"She worked very hard at fund-raising for charity, I gather," Mayo remarked, deliberately provocative.

"That!" The firelight caught the flash of scorn in her eyes. "That was nothing but one big ego-trip! Oh, I know, she could get blood out of a stone; how she did it's a mystery, but it was all for Fleur, wonderful Fleur, how selfless . . ." Abruptly she stopped. "There I go again."

But she'd succeeded in bringing to mind a file with long lists of names and the large amounts of money they'd donated. Names like Fennimore, Challis, Everard, and others—all well known locally. Also the scrapbook crammed with photographs of Fleur Saville handing over cheques, letters of thanks, laudatory newspaper clippings—and his own feeling of embarrassment when reading them. She added with a spurt of honesty, "Perhaps I'm not being fair. She did do an enormous amount of good. How she did it, God knows. Emotional blackmail, I suppose."

"And yet, despite appearances to the contrary, somebody may have had cause for a grudge against her? That's what you think? Can I ask you to be more specific?"

"You can, but I've said too much already. If I really went to town, there's no end to the people you might begin to suspect."

"One of them may be guilty."

"Yes. It might even be me, more than likely, on the evidence of what I've just said, mightn't it?" The look she slid him was assessing, and he wondered for a moment whether she was really clever, or just cunning, especially when she added, "God knows, what I've just said applies to a lot of people and they don't end up murdered, do they? I don't think even Fleur was that bad."

Despite her apparent frankness, he knew instinctively he couldn't trust her. She'd been quite right to say her opinions were not unbiased, and she'd lie without compunction if it suited her corner. She'd certainly lie to save Edwin Saville. And what about herself? How much of what she'd said was spite, how much truth? Did her dislike of Fleur amount to a willingness to get rid of her? He was quite convinced she would be morally capable of it, given the right circumstances. Physically capable, too. There were those strong, thin hands. She was slim, but used to hauling heavy furniture around. She had a van.

She also had no alibi, as it turned out. She readily confirmed Saville's statement about the time she was in his shop, though by now Mayo wasn't prepared to lay much store by that. The rest of the day she'd spent working on a small table she'd promised a client for Christmas.

"So you spent the whole of the rest of the afternoon here? Alone?"

"Alone in the afternoon and, alas, alone in the evening." She smiled her veiled smile again. He didn't respond.

Before he left, he paused at the door to ask one more question. He knew he needn't prevaricate with her, so he asked it outright.

"A *lover?*" The astounded look on her face gave him his answer; it almost, but not quite, gave way to a laugh. "I'm sorry, but you don't know how funny that is. Fleur? A lover? The only person Fleur Saville ever loved was Fleur Saville. No, Mr. Mayo, you're on the wrong tack there."

Mayo was still thinking about Zoe Henderson and what she'd said when, ten minutes later, as he reached Milford Road and the brightly lit car park of the police station, he spotted Alex going off duty. He waved and waited beside her car until she could reach it, the contrast between the two women, one so recently met and one so familiar, striking him forcibly. The one, malicious and having within her nature the capacity, if not the willingness, to destroy; the other so . . . but, as usual, when trying to define Alex, he was brought up short, and it occurred to him that even the way she was walking towards him, tall and slim-waisted, with a dancer's grace yet ever so slightly hesitant, was symbolic of her attitude towards him: eager, yet holding back, a barrier he couldn't ever quite break through.

"Gil, how's things?" she asked with a smile.

"Hardly started yet."

He didn't want to talk about the case. He'd had to make his apologies to her about the concert over the telephone, and as he'd expected, she'd made no fuss. She might ask her sister Lois to go with her, she'd said, take up the extra ticket. He said again now how sorry he was, still feeling he'd let her down badly. On the other hand, what could he do about it? Not a damn thing.

"It doesn't matter. Another time, hmm?"

Her expression was neutral, not conveying the usual matter-of-fact acceptance of the exigencies of his job, which she understood only too well, being in a better position than most to do so. She accepted without question that in this relationship, there was no place for the tears and recriminations that had eroded and worn away at the fabric of his marriage.

She swung her long legs into the driving seat and wound down the window, and he got a closer look at her face. "You all right, love?"

"Sure. I'm fine, why?"

"You don't look it."

She never had a great deal of colour; her complexion was naturally clear and pale, but today she seemed drained; there were smudges under those very dark blue eyes. In fact she looked washed-out. He might have put it down to the cold glare of the lighting where they stood, but it was more than that—there was a lassitude about her as well that was unusual. She admitted, "I just didn't seem to sleep very well last night for some reason."

"Have an early night tonight, then." He added carefully, watching her, "Wish I could do the same, but I'm likely to be here till God knows what time."

She smiled faintly, understanding what he meant, though perhaps not fully. Julie had gone back to her flat in Birmingham earlier than was strictly needful, before the end of her Christmas vacation, either using heavy-handed tact or more likely, as Mayo suspected, because there was a boy-friend of her own in the offing. His response to this was ambivalent. He liked to think of himself as a liberal-thinking parent, but he found he didn't much care for the implications of Julie's new emancipation. On the other hand, his own private life was restricted when she was at home, since he couldn't bring himself to come out with the true nature of his association with Alex. Not to his daughter, suspect what she might. He wasn't that kind of father, either.

Alex leaned forward out of the window and plucked a tiny piece of fluff from his lapel. He was suddenly conscious of his old jacket. Alex, always pin-neat herself, could make him feel a slob. Time he went shopping for a new jacket, only Lynne had bought this one for him, and somehow getting rid of it didn't seem right. Not just yet, anyway.

"I'll take your advice," she said.

"Think on, you do." Unexpectedly, he reached out to give her cheek the briefest of touches.

She watched him swing away and take the front steps of the building energetically, a tall man, straight and powerful, until he'd disappeared; then she slipped into gear and drove her car smoothly and expertly through the complicated one-way system of the town towards her flat. He would have been amazed if he had known what was going on inside her head, or even guessed at the increasingly desperate thoughts tumbling around there. She was afraid his patience must soon run out, and she couldn't blame him. It shouldn't be like this. I'm not being fair to him, she thought. What's *wrong* with me, for heavens sake? Why isn't it ever any good? And what am I going to do about it? Questions that never left her alone for very long these days.

Not entirely satisfied by Alex's reassurances, but unable to say why, Mayo put the niggle of worry to the back of his mind as he went inside. He paused by Atkins's desk, where the inspector sat drinking tea. All around him, telephones rang and were intercepted, typewriters clicked busily, computer screen cursors flashed continuously, but Atkins was oblivious, frowning at his typewriter, his pipe drawing furiously.

"Still here, George? Haven't you got a home to go to?"

Atkins put his mug down patiently on the counter, rested his pipe in the ashtray, and waited. The perfunctory nod he gave Mayo was his usual, universal method of greeting, nothing personal in it.

Mayo picked up the already typed sheets of Atkins's report, lying on his desk, and scanned it as best he could, making his way through the single-spaced, barely legible print, unsullied by any paragraph separations, few full stops, and no commas. He'd told George so many times to get a new ribbon in his typewriter and a dictionary and had been ignored, so he'd ceased to bother. He said,

"This Mrs. Tennyson and her daughter—did you send somebody to get their prints?"

"This afternoon."

"Anything useful I should know about either of them, before I see them?"

If there was anything, Atkins would know. Unambitiously but tirelessly plodding his way through until retirement, he had unplumbed depths of information on all sorts and conditions of people living in the borough of Lavenstock. It was just as quick, and frequently more enlightening, to ask him what you wanted to know than to run the questions through the computer. He never forgot a case. His work was his life and his love. It was rumoured at the station that his wife had had twins without his being aware she was expecting until after the event.

"Plenty," Atkins said, "and you'd better mind how you go. Not the size of two penn'orth o' copper, she isn't, but size has nothing to do with it."

"Like that, is it? One of our customers?"

"Not exactly, but she's been mixed up with some funny folk in her time. And that Kev of hers is a right pain. The girl's all right, though, and the youngest lad—he's at the Tech. Hear their ma's joined the Sally Army now—won't last long, few more weeks at most."

"You reckon?"

"Nothing else has, yet."

Mayo perched on the edge of the desk, and in the interests of encouraging Atkins to continue ignored the evilly smouldering pipe.

"Like this, see." Atkins proceeded to give Mayo a succinct, selective account of Lola Tennyson's varied and colourful activities: years ago, she'd been employed as a hostess at the Rose, the town's only so-called nightclub. "And you know what that means." That Kev of hers had been put on probation at thirteen . . . one of her live-in partners had regularly beaten her up and ended up doing time for GBH . . . she'd once kept a market stall selling second-hand clothes, toting them there in an old pram, until Kev had set

fire to the shed where she'd kept them with a tossed-away fag end
. . . "I won't go on. Want me to fix up a time for you to see her?"

Mayo's private opinion was that Mrs. Tennyson sounded more
sinned against than sinning. "No, best leave it and I'll sort it out
myself when it suits. Thanks, George."

Atkins nodded and took up his cooling tea.

8

Upstairs, Mayo found Kite ready with the information that Saville's account of his movements on the day his wife disappeared had been checked and found substantially correct. "Not that it helps him much. All in all," he remarked, "less than an hour of his afternoon is accounted for."

"Anything yet on Mrs. Saville's movements?"

"Not a dicky-bird so far. Nobody seems to have seen her since she left the hall at twelve-thirty that Saturday—none of those helpers we've already seen, that is. Which is all of them, except Mrs. Pound the vicar's wife, Mrs. Fennimore, and Mrs. Challis."

"Mrs. Challis the J.P. ?"

"Yes. She lives out at Lattimer Wood, so I rang first, but there's been no answer all day. And Mrs. Fennimore set off this afternoon to baby-sit for their daughter, and won't be home until late tonight. Mrs. Pound was out as well; it was the vicar who gave me the names of the helpers. None of them saw her after they finished at half-twelve. There's two sisters, though, Miss Amy and Miss Violet Wood, who were a bit more helpful. They couldn't say why, exactly, but they thought she seemed a bit strange that morning. They're a couple of old ducks who obviously thought the sun shone out of her, but they're a bit vague, and the nearest either of them could come to it was that she seemed preoccupied. Not quite like her usual dear self, was how they put it."

Kite had interviewed the two old ladies himself. Had they noticed if she was wearing her rings, he'd enquired, a point that Mayo had specifically wished to be raised.

"Her rings?" repeated Amy, the vague, sweet-faced one, shaking her head.

"Of course she was wearing her wedding ring—and I'm quite

sure the pretty ruby and diamond one as well," asserted Violet, the one who used make-up. "I always notice people's jewellery—and their hands. Such nice hands she had." Looking complacently at her own, still white and unblotched with the spots of age, heavily encumbered with sapphires and diamonds winking in old-fashioned gold settings.

"Not much to go on, is it?" Mayo commented.

"But it seems to confirm she went home."

"So it would seem." Mayo was non-committal. "What else have we turned up?"

Kite summarised the various reports relating to Saville's alibi, collected from the D.C.'s detailed to make the enquiries, for Mayo's benefit. "First there's Mr. Howe, the head of the Comprehensive. He went into the shop that Saturday, just as Saville was opening up at half-two, and left about five to three without buying anything. He was watching the time, because his parking was due to run out just after the hour. Then the other customer, a girl by the name of Janet Rainbow, from Branxmore, called to collect the map Saville had had framed for her. She works at Tixall's Estate Agents, and I sent Deeley to see her. She told him she dashed in to pick up the map—it was a Christmas present for her dad—but she'd no idea of the time. Mr. Howe recalls her coming in as he left, though. She used to be one of his pupils, and they exchanged the compliments of the season. She was in the shop only as long as it took to wrap the parcel and pay for it—probably abut five or ten minutes."

"What about the woman at the shop next door?"

"Mrs. Wilson at the Baker's Dozen? I saw her myself. She went to ask Saville about parking her car in his yard, a minute or two after one o'clock—"

"I thought he said it was just before two-thirty?" Mayo interrupted sharply.

"That was the second time. The first time was about five past one, but he'd already locked up—and there was no answer when she knocked. He could've been trying to pull a fast one there, saying he never went out all through lunch-time."

"Not necessarily. He hardly strikes me as the sort to open up when he's taking his lunch break, especially if he knew who it was. He made it plain he finds her a nuisance."

"That makes two of them—I mean, she doesn't care for him, either, I'd guess, though she was careful not to say so. She thought better of his wife. Lovely lady, Mrs. Saville, she said. In fact, everybody we've spoken to so far seems to have had a good word for her."

"I daresay. Sinners have a funny habit of becoming saints once they're dead, and vice-versa, haven't you noticed? It was half past two, as Saville said, when she tried again, Mrs. Wilson?"

"Just before. She wouldn't have asked him at all, she says, only she couldn't find anywhere else to park. Her own little yard only has room for the shop's delivery van. She was on about the lack of parking round there, and I must agree, it's getting more chaotic by the day—"

"They'd have enough to say if they got a multi-storey car park shoved up bang in the middle of their trendy nostalgia," Mayo remarked, intercepting the telephone on its second ring. "Mayo here."

"Glad I've caught you, Chief Inspector," came Timpson-Ludgate's rich, fruity voice, his equilibrium apparently restored after the shock to his social system. "Thought you'd like to know what I've found."

"Already! You've been quick off the mark!"

"Knew you'd be anxious to know. Besides, old son, I'm hopefully off tonight to Austria for a spot of skiing—" Ah, Mayo thought cynically, all was explained. But he wasn't grumbling; if it hadn't been for Timpson-Ludgate's holiday, he wouldn't have had his report this early. "That is, if you don't find any more murders for me."

"Murder, was it, then?"

"Let's put it this way—injuries like that are neither self-inflicted nor accidental. You'll be having my official report later, but I can tell you now that death was due to a subdural haemorrhage—"

"Keep it simple, please."

Timpson-Ludgate gave a grunt of amusement. "She died from a' blow to the left temple."

"Not a fall?"

"No, a single, direct blow."

"What kind of object are we looking for? Heavy? Blunt?"

"Sharp—not necessarily heavy, but applied with considerable force. I wouldn't like to say what, but I'd say something with a sharp, right-angled corner, something with a certain thickness to it. Possibly metal, since I found no splinters or fragments of any kind. I can also tell you she may have been left curled up for some hours before she was dumped where she was found."

"In a car boot, for instance?"

"Very likely."

"Time of death?"

"Ah, well, now. All you've got to do is find out when she had her last meal. This Arctic weather we've been having did a good job for us, preserving her like that, so it's possible to tell she died within a couple of hours of eating. Bread and cheese, practically undigested."

Mayo's own stomach churned as he reflected for a second on the horrible aspects of the pathologist's job. "Couple of hours, you say? That's interesting. Well, thank you for your trouble. I'm sorry it's thawing; I hope they don't have to use the snow-machines in Austria. Enjoy yourself."

"That's what I'm paid for. The trouble, I mean. Cheers." Mayo put the phone down.

"You heard that. All the stops out now, Martin. We've got a murder on our hands."

Kite grunted. "What's new? I mean, we always knew that, didn't we?"

"I've no objection to having it confirmed, all the same. There was always the outside chance of an accident." Mayo went on to repeat the rest of the pathologist's finding to a now attentive Kite.

Kite said, "That makes it between, say, about one o'clock and three when she died—assuming she went straight home from the church hall and ate her lunch."

Quite possible, then, for Saville to have killed her. Saville, their only suspect so far, one with a probable motive and maybe the opportunity. But Mayo remembered the conviction he'd had at

Kelsey Road that Fleur Saville hadn't died in her own home. With nothing to support an intuition that the reasons for Fleur Saville's death weren't that simple, an instinct that this wasn't how it had happened, he said, "A big 'if,' that. We've nothing to show that she did in fact go home, yet."

"Except the jewellery she left behind."

Mayo rubbed a hand down the length of his face. It had been a long day. Only twelve hours since the case had broken, but twelve hours on the go, with only the odd snatched sandwich in between all the work that went into setting up the machinery of an enquiry into a death in mysterious circumstances. A death that was now officially murder. Deeper investigations. Nets that would have to be spread wider.

What, for instance, about the dead woman herself? He took the photo Nell Fennimore had left from his desk drawer and studied it. Had she been the woman pictured by Zoe Henderson? Or one talented, highly thought of, the tireless worker for good causes, liked and admired by all? Leading a blameless life, with nothing to hide? He was inclined—he'd go no further than that at the moment —to reserve judgement on the latter. But anyone, for God's sake, as pathologically tidy as Fleur Saville surely had something to hide— unless someone had deliberately tidied away all traces of her. Maybe her papers would tell them something about her? They were there, waiting to be gone through. Tonight.

He could feel himself sagging in his chair. He needed a shot in the arm: a good meal and a drink, relaxation with a book maybe— reading, as well as music, was a deep pleasure for him. He thought of Alex, alone in her flat . . . diversions and digressions . . .

"Come on, Sherlock," he said, indicating the parcel of Fleur Saville's correspondence and files on the table in the corner. "Sooner we get moving, sooner we see our beds."

Kite stifled a cracking yawn and ran a hand through his hair. "Some coffee and a couple of rounds of sandwiches before we begin, all right?" he stipulated.

Mayo agreed. "It'll give us time to get our second wind, but for the love of Mike let's go downstairs and get something hot." Even the canteen egg and chips—or in Mayo's own case, a boring and virtuous omelette—was preferable to another goddam sandwich.

It was past ten when Mayo got home. He showered and went straight to bed with a glass of scotch and the latest Fleur Lamont, *Salamander Fire*, said to be her best, to keep him company. He found it colourful and highly inventive, suggestive rather than explicit, and ultimately boring. He tried to persevere with it, but with limited success, managing only to get to page thirty-five before dropping off, the book sliding from his fingers.

He didn't expect to find Saville at his shop the following morning, but he made the bookshop in Butter Lane his first call and did in fact find him there, checking through a pile of catalogues in the back room in a fug of heat from the gas fire and a bubbling coffee percolator. He decided Saville was going to need that coffee, and before making the purpose of his visit known he accepted the offer to join him.

"Have you read all these?" Mayo asked while the other man poured the fierce black brew. He waved towards the piles of books that had gravitated from the shop proper into the space at the back, which, he thought with sudden insight, even more than Kelsey Road, was the place where Saville was at home, his own personal space, what he understood, and maybe his solace.

"A good percentage. I find the study of the criminal mind endlessly fascinating, as you yourself must. You've bought from me occasionally, haven't you?" It was the first time Saville had acknowledged recognition. He gave a brief, bleak smile. "But that isn't what you came to see me about, is it?"

"No, sir, I'm afraid it isn't."

Saville sat motionless and silent after the manner of his wife's death had been imparted to him. At last he spoke. "After the circumstances in which she was found, I can't pretend it's entirely unexpected. Nevertheless, it's a blow." A look of bitter resignation had settled on his face. Shock, if shock there had been in the first instance, had given way to an apparently quite genuine grief, though this didn't rule out, as far as Mayo was concerned, the possibility of the man having murdered his wife. He could still have loved her deeply, even if he'd done away with her, perhaps because of it. In a momentary loss of control, or at the end of his tether, perhaps through jealousy. The quarrel maybe arousing a killer instinct which had lain dormant, unsuspected, for years . . . these quiet ones, the deep sort, they were often the worst. When they flew off the handle, they did it properly.

Yes, there were all the ingredients of a classic domestic murder, except that Mayo was still having trouble believing it. It was wrong in his head. And, usually so sure of himself, he was bothered because he didn't know why.

"Are you arresting me?" Saville asked suddenly. His face had a grey tinge, like unrisen dough.

"No, sir." Mayo didn't enlarge. Saville must realise that they had ample grounds for suspicion and might be fishing as to whether they'd yet found anything more damaging. It wouldn't do any harm to let him sweat a bit.

He sat on a high, old-fashioned stool before his cluttered table, his shoulders bowed, his face hidden. "There was no need for it," he said unexpectedly, looking up. "I shall never forgive myself."

Mayo swallowed a mouthful of coffee, burning his tongue. "Forgive yourself?"

"Don't get me wrong; I'm not making a confession. That's not what I mean." A corner of his mouth had lifted, seeing the effect of his words. Maybe a sense of the ironic lurked somewhere under that humourless exterior, after all. "I mean that she had her faults —who doesn't? But she was good, a good wife, a good woman. I shouldn't have entertained the thoughts I did about her—but it was the jewellery," he said, coming to a point that troubled Mayo also, "how to explain that? If she was killed by an intruder—" He stopped short, meeting Mayo's disbelief. "No, that won't do either, will it? No casual intruder would have taken her away like that, or left her valuables. But it's unthinkable that anyone she knew could have done it!"

They all said that. It wasn't usually how it turned out, however, rather the opposite.

"I've asked you before, Mr. Saville, but now you've had time to think, I'll ask again—you know of no-one who had a grudge against her, however slight?"

"She hadn't an enemy in the world."

They often said that, too, though he wondered if this, in its strictest sense, could ever be said of anyone. Mayo said abruptly, "You haven't been honest with me; you haven't told me everything you know about what happened the day your wife disappeared, have you?"

Saville had a prominent Adam's apple, which worked convulsively. He shook his head, denying the allegation. Mayo knew he was lying.

On the long trestle table under the window, amongst a great deal of messy, extraneous junk, were the catalogues Saville had been working on, also a small but weighty picture frame, heavily gilded and embossed, also a saucepan containing the dried-up remains of a tin of baked beans, and some burnt toast. Not a man to make out for himself, Edwin Saville. But Mayo, thinking guiltily of the state of his own kitchen on occasions, wasn't in any position to cast stones and didn't pursue the thought.

"It's not always good to be alone at times like this, sir. Isn't there anyone who could stay with you? No member of your family—a son or daughter?" The closed, shut-in look that Mayo had come to know so well returned to Saville's face.

"Fleur and I had no children."

"I see." Mayo stood up to leave and took the opportunity to have a better look at the picture frame. Right-angled, easily held in the hand, heavyish-looking. The sort of object Fleur Saville might have been killed with. He picked it up, and brief ideas about it being the murder weapon disappeared. It was a sham, made of plastic, light and insubstantial, and no threat to anyone. He found himself wondering if this could also be true of the owner.

Saville held out his hand to take the frame back, his left hand. He'd held his coffee-mug also in his left hand, Mayo had noticed. The blow which had killed his wife had been on her left temple, and it was odds-on, though by no means certain, that her killer had been right-handed.

9

Nell Fennimore sat hunched on the cushioned window seat, staring dismally through swollen eyelids at the dreary, foggy prospect outside the window. Saturday morning, and the world was looking and feeling like a smudged pen-and-ink drawing done on coarse grey wrapping-paper. Her face was blotched, her handkerchief screwed into a tight, damp ball; preparations for lunch weren't even started, although it was well after midday and Gerald would soon be in. She felt she had never known such pain and misery.

Obscurely, she blamed the weather for everything that had happened. If it hadn't been for the snow, poor darling Fleur wouldn't have lain there undiscovered all that time. There were going to be questions: Why? What in the world had she been doing out there at Seton End at all? What had *happened* to her? Nell's mind veered away, not wanting to face the implications. Oh heavens, it was all so *awful*. And how odd of Edwin not to have let her know until today. More than that, very nearly unpardonable.

Added to which Gerald, normally so amenable, so understanding, had not, today of all days, been in the sweetest of tempers. Deprived for two weeks of his usual three daily miles of jogging, he'd unwisely attempted it this morning, seeing that the thaw was well underway, an undertaking anyone might have told him was fraught with peril. Splashed and spattered, cursed by passing motorists for impeding what was still a narrow passage between banks of traffic-blackened slush, he'd returned home disgruntled and impatient.

And when the news, the unspeakable, dreadful news, about Fleur had come . . . he'd been horrified, yes. And lovingly supportive, as always. But his sympathy hadn't seemed *entirely* wholehearted. He was still ruffled, even a bit short at being interrupted between appointments with the news. Though on reflection that was perhaps understandable. Saturday mornings were dedicated to private patients.

Preoccupied by her misery, she didn't hear him come in. The first intimation that he was there was when she felt his arms around her, his chin nuzzling into the back of her neck. "Sorry, Nellie-Nell, sorry if I was a bit offhand." The silly lover's nickname made her turn a woebegone face to him, and she saw his equanimity was restored, his capacity for comfort and reassurance back in place. "My poor darling."

"Nothing's going to be the same again." She felt a sob rise in her throat, the sting of fresh tears behind her eyelids.

"I know."

He held her against him, pressing her head against his shoulder, strong and solid. But he didn't know—nobody could know—the loss. "She was so good," she hiccuped, "so sweet. What am I going to do without her?"

He saw her memories were already becoming exaggerated and distorted, and might grow increasingly so, hallowed by the manner of Fleur's death, having little in common with the reality of Fleur's nature, if he didn't put a stop to it. He couldn't bring himself, however, to disillusion her. Not at this point, perhaps never.

A car drew into the drive. A man got out. "Dry your eyes, Nellie-Nell, dear. We have a visitor."

Kite was shown into the sitting room at the back of the house, a large and pleasant, though not very tidy room, decorated for cheerfulness and comfort rather than taste, full of books and a large woolly dog of uncertain age, sex, and pedigree which occupied most of the hearth rug.

"I hope I'm not interrupting your work, or your lunch," he said politely to the Fennimores, though basically he wouldn't have allowed it to make any difference.

"Not at all, I finish surgery at twelve-thirty on Saturdays."

"And lunch won't be much today."

Mrs. Fennimore hadn't been able to erase the signs of recent tears, but she had blown her nose and dried her eyes and generally made an effort to pull herself together, Kite could tell. He tried to show her that he wasn't about to put her through an ordeal. "I shan't keep you long," he told her, in a friendly manner intended to put her at her ease. "You already gave my chief a very clear and straightforward picture up to lunch-time on the day Mrs. Saville disappeared. But there are one or two other things which have cropped up."

"Such an understanding man, your chief inspector." Kite was taken aback. It wasn't the kind of compliment that often came Mayo's way. It was usually a long time before people got to know him well enough to realise there was at least a grain of truth in this. Mrs. Fennimore was not quite so ingenuous as she first seemed. He coughed and opened his notebook. To begin with, did she know a Mr. Kenneth Anstruther or a Mr. David Garbett?

"I've never heard of either. Who are they?"

"They're partners in the Broadfield Garden Centre, where I understand Mrs. Saville was in the habit of buying flowers."

"Oh, I know those two, yes, if they're the two men who are always around in the shop, though I don't think I've ever heard their names. I used to drive Fleur down there nearly every Friday to pick up flowers for the weekend." Tears threatened again, and she had to swallow hard before she could go on. "But what have they to do with Fleur?"

"Her body was found quite close to the cottage where they live. It was Mr. Anstruther, in fact, who found her."

"Oh dear, poor man, how ghastly for him! But you can't mean— no, of course you don't. She didn't know them any better than I did." She said nothing more for a moment, and then, raising clear hazel eyes to his, asked quietly, unexpectedly, "Sergeant, how exactly did Fleur die?"

There was no reason why she shouldn't know, no way he could wrap it up. He gave it to her straight, and to his relief she didn't burst into sobs or have hysterics. "Yes," she said, barely audible, "I thought that's what you were going to say." Her husband reached out for her hand, and she held on to it as though it were a lifeline. "Go on, please. What else do you want to know?"

"About this quarrel Mrs. Tennyson overheard, between Mrs. Saville and her husband. It was unusual, I gather?"

"They never had a wrong word," Nell replied with conviction and then flushed. "As far as I know, of course." Kite could see the struggle she was having between her conscience and her regret that she'd been the one to bring the row to the attention of the police. "But Lola, you know—Mrs. Tennyson—she has a tendency to dramatise. She *could* have been mistaken."

Not in this case, though, Kite thought, on Saville's own admission the row had taken place. And Nell Fennimore herself had believed Mrs. Tennyson to the extent of reporting it. But he held his peace, merely asking what he'd asked of all the other helpers, "Would you say Mrs. Saville behaved quite normally that morning? In no way out of the ordinary? Not obviously upset or anything?"

"Naturally, I've thought about that, over and over, since Lola told me. If Fleur and Edwin had quarrelled, Fleur would certainly have been very upset indeed, but I can't honestly say I noticed anything. We *were* very busy, though, I have to admit. They wouldn't let us have the hall before half past ten, because there'd been a dance the night before and they had to clean up, so we had all our work cut out and not much time to chat."

"I see. And when you left her, what did she say?"

"She didn't say anything; she just put her hand up and waved. I was rushing off, you see, to meet Gerald. We had a few last-minute presents to buy, and I was first out. After we'd finished the shopping and I'd picked up Fleur's prescription, we had lunch together before I went back, didn't we, darling?"

Fennimore nodded confirmation. "At the White Cat, the cafe in Sheep Street."

"So you weren't actually there when Mrs. Saville left?" Nell shook her head.

"I understand she didn't have a car, but it's not far to Kelsey Road, so presumably she'd have walked?"

Nell almost smiled at that. "Fleur hated walking anywhere. No, she wouldn't have done that. It was a foul day anyway. One of the others would be sure to have given her a lift home."

"Did she have a handbag with her?"

"Well, of course. She wouldn't go out without one, would she?"

"Did you notice what sort?"

For a moment Nell looked blank. "Black patent," she said eventually. "I didn't notice it particularly, but it would be—to go with her shoes. She was very fussy about things like that—not like me; I tend to use this all-purpose one nearly all the time."

The one she indicated was lying on the floor beside one of the chairs. Kite had seen them advertised as 'organiser' bags, more like a briefcase than a handbag, he thought; the way this one bulged, it didn't look very organised.

"Or it's possible," Nell went on, "that somebody may have asked her home to lunch. She was never short of invitations. She was that sort of person, you see—fun to have around, very popular with everybody."

"Except young Michael," Fennimore put in and immediately looked as though he wished he hadn't.

"Oh, Gerald, that was years ago!" What was the matter with him today? Nell bit her lip and looked apprehensively at Kite, as if he might think Gerald was implying that Michael might have had something to do with Fleur dying, which was ridiculous. The sergeant looked at first sight to be very youthful for his rank, but his bright blue eyes were shrewd and sharp when they weren't smiling, and she suspected that anybody who underestimated him might be making a big mistake.

"Who's Michael?"

"Edwin's son," she got in quickly, thinking she'd put things in a better light than Gerald, "by his first marriage. Michael adored his mother and she died when he was very young, so it wasn't all that surprising he resented Fleur rather when Edwin married her soon after. You know what that sort of situation can be like."

"She didn't help by packing him off to school—that was a tactical error. But I'm bound to admit," Fennimore added, trying fairly obviously to make up for his earlier incautious remark, "that she did try to do her best with him after he left school and came home to live, though by then it was probably too late. Michael at that age would have tried the patience of a saint. It was maybe just as well he left home, though it was a pity it happened the way it did."

"Packed up and left after a row, did he?"

"How did you guess?" Nell asked.

"It's not unusual; you'd be surprised. What was the row about?"

Fennimore spread his hands. "He demanded some of the money his mother had left—she came from a wealthy family—in order to go off and 'do his own thing,' shake the dust of Lavenstock off his feet, and find enlightenment in India or wherever the young were going then. Fleur persuaded Edwin not to let him have the money, and quite right, too. The phase he was going through, he'd probably have given it all to some hippie commune or other, the young fool. But a lot of bad feeling was generated."

"Where is he now?"

Husband and wife exchanged glances. "Blowed if I know. Haven't seen him for—oh, seven or eight years, I suppose. Nell?"

"I've no idea where he is. It was something Fleur preferred to forget, and Edwin never mentioned him. The whole thing made him very unhappy."

"It aged him ten years, poor devil," Fennimore said bluntly. "And it's not hard to understand why. Michael was frankly a pain in the neck, as they often are at that age, and Fleur . . . well, old Edwin must have felt like the meat in the sandwich."

Fennimore, out of consideration for his wife no doubt, was saying less than he might have done on the subject of Fleur Saville, Kite was sure. Otherwise it might not have occurred to Kite to ask him, too, what he'd been doing with himself that afternoon after he left his wife outside the church hall.

"Me? Oh, nothing much. I took Bismarck here out for a walk round the park and then came home and went spark out in front of the box. There was no match on because of the weather, only an old film that was so boring I fell asleep."

Bismarck! thought Kite, looking at the amiable old bundle of smelly fur, which had pricked up its ears at its name and the word "walk." How extraordinary people are about their dogs.

Mayo allowed himself to succumb at lunch-time to the steak and kidney when he and Kite met for lunch in the Saracen's. He was up to here with salad, and the savoury smell of their renowned dish had been too much for him—and anyway, the waistband of his trousers was already noticeably looser. "Cheers," he said, lifting his pint. "How d'you get on with Mrs. Fennimore?"

"She hadn't a lot more to tell me than she told you in the first place, not about the twenty-second . . . but I did find out an interesting thing or two. First, he's been married before—"

"Who has? Saville?" Mayo put down his glass and stared at Kite. "Well, well. He's a bit of a dark horse, isn't he? Married twice, and with another attractive woman in tow!" He'd learned the date of Saville's marriage to Fleur, but it hadn't occurred to him to ask about a previous one, for the simple but not excusable reason that Saville had to him all the appearance of a confirmed bachelor succumbing late to the married state. Yet his type was often attractive to a certain sort of woman: competent, self-motivated, often childless women who rather liked the idea of an apparently helpless man dependant on them—like Zoe Henderson, for instance. Into his mind too came the memory of that fleeting, attractive smile of Saville's. In his younger days, Mayo conceded, he could have been quite a handsome man.

"Also, he has a son by his first marriage who had a grudge against his stepmamma." Kite repeated what the Fennimores had told him, enjoying the effect on Mayo.

"The old devil! Only this morning he told me he had no children." Or rather, he corrected himself, Saville had implied it by the manner in which he'd phrased his answer to the question, saying—quite truthfully, Mayo supposed—that he and Fleur were childless. "Any other little gems like that, have you?"

Kite looked complacent, but shook his head. "It all happened years ago, anyway, and Michael—the son—hasn't been seen or heard of for ten or eleven years."

Mayo made no comment, staring at the now-brittle sprigs of holly that decorated the top of each picture set against the flock-papered walls, the tinsel draped around the bar, while talk and laughter from the Saturday lunch-time crowds rose and fell around them. It was long odds on the boy having come back after all these years to murder his stepmother, but any lead was worth following up. Especially since it was the only sniff they'd had so far of anyone other than Saville—and maybe Zoe Henderson—with even the glimmer of a motive. A large man with a shiny red face and a padded cotton jerkin cannoned into their table, spilling a few drops from the clutch of gin and tonics in Mayo's hand, blundering on without apology. Mayo wiped them off absently. "That sounds like ours, Martin."

The Saracen's Head had a system at lunch-times that would have lost them Mayo's custom had it not been for the excellence of its food, of giving you a number when you ordered your meal, and calling it out when the food was ready. Kite came back from the bar, bearing two steaming plates and cutlery wrapped in paper napkins.

While they consumed the pie, Mayo said, "I managed to have a word with Mrs. Saville's solicitor this morning. Those books she wrote must have been hot property in more ways than one. She was worth a mint."

"And who benefits?"

"According to her will, Saville. Gets every penny. Plus insurances."

"Does he, by gum? And Gerald Fennimore said his first wife was wealthy, too."

"To lose one wife in circumstances where you're likely to benefit may be regarded as a misfortune, but to lose two . . ."

"Looks deliberate?"

"Quite. I don't know, though. Isn't it a bit too obvious?"

"You're the one who always says the obvious choice is usually the right one."

Mayo inspected the cruet and selected more English mustard.

"Well, how many more motives do we want?" Kite demanded. "She was trying to force him into something he didn't want to do, they quarrelled, she's left him money, *as did his first wife* . . . his time that day isn't wholly accounted for."

Kite pushed his empty plate away, drained his glass, and got ready to leave. "I'd give a lot to know a bit more about this first marriage of Saville's. I don't believe in coincidences."

"Dig around. I wouldn't be averse to knowing, myself," Mayo said mildly. "And if I were you, I would start with Jim Sutcliffe at the *Advertiser*. Arrange for us to have a word. But at the moment it's more important to find out where—and when—Mrs. Saville ate her lunch, to give us a more precise time of death. You'd better concentrate on the vicar's wife and Mrs. Challis, find out if either of them gave her a lift home or whatever."

Kite was still unable to contact Mrs. Challis, but late afternoon found him waiting in the parish church for Jennifer Pound, the vicar's wife, to finish arranging the flowers on the altar for the next day.

"Hang about; shan't keep you waiting long, Mr. Kite," she said cheerfully.

The Pounds were a young couple, the subject of enjoyable specu-lation and controversy amongst the older, staider, and more shock-able of the parishioners of St. Nicholas. He was unorthodox and didn't even wear a dog collar, and some of them wondered some-times if perhaps they hadn't stumbled into a country-and-western show by mistake, expecting a service, what with the swinging tunes to the hymns, accompanied on occasions by the vicar's wife on the guitar. Today she was wearing jeans, tucked into high leather boots, and a leather jacket. She called herself "Ms." and taught the Kite children at the local junior school.

"I assume it is me you want to talk to and not my husband? Not in a hurry, are you?"

She thought he'd come to talk about Davey, who was usually in hot water of some kind.

"Finish what you're doing, Mrs. Pound."

He stood awkwardly watching her as she moved about between the altar and the vestry, substituting the fresh daffodils and tulips she'd brought for the ones already in the big brass ewers. She didn't seem to be making a very good job of it to Kite, who was admittedly no expert. The ones she was throwing away had appeared perfectly fresh, though perhaps they wouldn't have lasted through the following week, and they'd been artistically arranged, which hers were not. Her bottom was neat and round in the tight jeans every time she bent down, and he primly averted his eyes and stood, stiff and awkward, waiting. He didn't want to sit in one of the front pews, where he'd have to shout to make himself heard, and didn't know whether it would be taking too great a liberty to sit anywhere else. It was a long time since he'd last been in church, and that was for a wedding.

She finished what she was doing and solved his dilemma by slipping into one of the choir stalls and beckoning him to join her. "Now, what is it you wanted to see me about?"

When he'd finished telling her, she sat silently for a moment, biting her lip. "How crass of me. I'm so sorry, I should have known what you were here for. Such a shock it was to hear about her. She'll be a terrible loss to the whole community. How—how did she die?"

"We believe she was murdered."

She uttered a small, shocked expression. "Did you know her well?" Kite asked.

Mrs. Pound hesitated. "Not *well*. In fact I hardly knew her, only in so far as her work for the church and charity, especially the Buttercup Club, was concerned. She'll be dreadfully missed in that direction. Aside from her work, I believe that was the one thing in her life she cared about most. There was a reason for it, of course. She confided in me once that she had had a child who was born terribly disabled and died in his first year."

"What do you know about her husband? Is he a churchgoer?"

"No, they always seemed to lead rather separate lives. But," she added hastily, "you don't have to be in each other's pockets all day to be close, you know. From all I've heard, they were devoted."

"You've never heard any rumours about her—about another man?"

She looked at him, astounded. "Fleur Saville wouldn't get up to those sort of tricks!"

Where had she been, all her thirty-five or so years, this enlightened wife of the vicarage, that she didn't know that *anybody* was likely to get up to tricks like that, even vicars' wives? She must have read his look, however, because she pulled a face and said a trifle shamefacedly, "No, I don't really know, do I? But I honestly don't think so."

Kite went on to ask her about the children's party. Like the rest of the women interviewed, she didn't appear to have noticed anything unusual about Fleur's behaviour that morning. She said again, "I don't know what we're going to do without her, though I suppose Gillian Challis will be willing enough to take over the Buttercup Club; they more or less ran it together. In fact . . ." She broke off what she'd been going to say, as if she'd thought better of it.

"Challis?" Kite asked. "The Mrs. Challis who lives out at Lattimer Wood? We still have to see her. She was out when I rang earlier."

"I was the last to leave that lunch-time because I had to lock up, and I'm almost certain I heard Gillian offering Fleur a lift home. They were very close friends. She's your best bet; she'll be able to help you more than I've done in every way."

"People who are not quite so close are often better able to give a less subjective view, Mrs. Pound."

"Well, I'm not one of them, not in this case. Look, I don't mean to be unco-operative, but as I said, I didn't know her well. In fact I —never felt quite at ease with her; I don't know why. She had this beautiful speaking voice, very soft and melodious and persuasive. Somehow, you found yourself doing what she wanted, sometimes against your will. She was so good, and yet—there was something about her I didn't—" She broke off and looked at Kite with very round, very blue eyes.

"Didn't like?"

"Not—exactly. Didn't understand, I think." She looked uneasy. For all her emancipation, he could see she still felt the old taboo about disrespect to the dead. "She put her name to all these fund-raising efforts, but my husband, well, he used to think it was all rather well staged to give her the limelight. He used, I'm afraid, to call her 'Our Star Performer.' " She blushed vividly. "I think you'd better forget I said that."

Kite thought that Mrs. Pound, despite all her efforts to the contrary, hadn't succeeded in losing her natural ingenuousness.

10

"And now for Mrs. Justice of the Peace Challis. Got your bullet-proof vest on, Martin? The lady doesn't suffer fools gladly—though one thing's certain," Mayo added with a short laugh, "we'll get a straight answer."

They were driving out together to see Mrs. Challis, whom Mayo had come across several times in the course of his duty. He'd read the forceful, downright letters she wrote to the *Advertiser*, too, and respected what he'd seen of her brisk, no-nonsense manner. She could be ruthless with offenders when the occasion demanded it, largely because, he imagined, she expected everyone to have as much integrity as she undoubtedly had herself. Her trouble was that she saw everything strictly in black and white; there was never room for grey areas, and this unwavering conviction of the rightness of her judgements made her unpopular with certain sections of the community. Despite this, Mayo felt he'd rather deal with her than some of her woolly-minded colleagues. You knew where you were with her.

The church bells were ringing from the parish church as they left and took the Birmingham road towards Lattimer Wood. Kite drove and Mayo watched people going about their business, fetching newspapers, guiding children on Christmas-present bicycles over bumpy pavements, or even—though it was still drizzling—joining the enthusiastic army of Sunday morning car washers. In Branxmore, where there was only on-street parking, and you had to hose down your car in the street, there was much evidence of this. In the suburbs of Tannersley and Henchard, out towards Lattimer Wood, in the snooty part where town gave way to country, any such labour was discreetly hidden behind trees and shrubs in quarter-acre lots. The Challis house lay even beyond this, in open country with no visible neighbours and a sweeping drive a quarter of a mile long.

The road to Lattimer Wood led though the Seton End cross-roads. Seton Lodge, as they passed, looked as prim and self-contained, as slightly unreal as ever, but the lane where the body had stayed undiscovered under two feet of snow had been reduced by the tramping feet of many policemen to a sea of grey slush, closed at the entrance by a red and white barrier.

Anstruther, as the unlucky finder of the body, would have to appear at the inquest, which was scheduled for Tuesday, but Mayo was fairly satisfied in his own mind that he'd had nothing to do with the murder. Both he and his partner Garbett had been provided with satisfactory alibis by their staff, with whom they'd been working the whole of that Saturday, and also for the early evening by other guests at the party they'd attended; there seemed, moreover, to be no known connections between either of them and the dead woman.

But *why there?* Mayo had asked himself more than once. Why had that particular spot been chosen to dump the body? Not the lane— the murderer wouldn't have had any choice but to leave the body where he did, if he was making for the gravel pits. It was dangerous dumping it, in full view of the headlights of any car coming from the direction of Birmingham, with that bend in the road, but on the other hand he couldn't have risked pressing on and getting stuck in a snowdrift. Mayo himself had seen how the lane degenerated, on the morning when the body was discovered, when he and Kite had tramped a partly cleared path through the snow to view the deep waterfilled pits. But why the gravel pits in the first place?

"Who'd be likely to know where that lane led, Martin?" Kite would probably know; he was a local man, born and bred in the area.

"Practically anybody . . . folks exercise their dogs on that heathland. Or anybody else could have known, for that matter— it's a convenient spot to draw off the road for a break if you're driving, attractive in the summertime. And, as Deeley said, courting couples. It's accessible enough at most times. Those pits aren't fenced off or anything, though they should be, even with the trespass warnings there. There was a case last year when some kids were fooling around and one of them fell in and nearly drowned. There was talk of prosecution, to make an example. Caused a lot of outrage."

As a method of concealment, then, it lacked at least the main requirement—that of permanently disposing of the body. Sooner or later, it would have surfaced, and been spotted. Which was perhaps another point in Saville's favour. Would he, a student of criminology, have ignored this basic fact?

The Challis House, long and low, was of mellow stone with a red-pantiled roof and lattice windows, huge stone urns beside the door lavishly planted with purple and yellow winter-flowering pansies, looking at the moment slightly battered. The only response to the hollow reverberations of the iron lion-faced knocker on the heavy oak door was the frantic, prolonged Hound-of-the-Baskerville baying of a dog from somewhere inside the house. Somewhere a long way off. Boxwinder House had until fairly recently been a large farmhouse, with its origins in Tudor times.

"They may be away for the weekend," Kite remarked, "with somebody coming in to look after the dog."

"We'll wait."

"There's been no answer to the telephone for a couple of days."

Mayo's only reply was a grunt, and Kite gave up and followed him back to the car, where they sat gazing out in silence. To their right, a paddock occupied by two damp and dejected ponies who were ignoring the open door of a timbered stable in the corner. In front of them, a big secluded garden, landscaped with clusters of deciduous shrubs and trees and dark, glossy rhododendrons, where a summerhouse and tennis court, and a swimming pool under a cover lay partly obscured by the grey moisture dripping onto the slowly melting snow. Freezing conditions were forecast for the night, unfortunately likely to prolong the thaw even further.

"Ever come across Challis, Martin?" Mayo enquired conversationally.

"Not personally. We don't move in the same circles."

"Where's he get his money for all this?" Mayo went on, ignoring the sarcasm. "Where does anybody, for that matter?"

"Public school and Oxford, Rugby Blue, went down without taking his degree, but straight into his father's City firm—that's Browne Moulton, the merchant bankers, very top-drawer. He commutes every day—by car, not train," Kite recited rapidly, very pleased with himself at being able to score by having asked around, until he saw Mayo's grin and realised the questions had been rhetorical; he'd known all along.

"His public school was Ampleforth," Mayo enlarged, infuriatingly.

"So?" Kite was casual, trying not to show his discomfiture.

"R.C. that, isn't it? So they'll likely be at Mass. Not bloomin' heathens, like us lot, you know, the Catholics." Relenting, Mayo explained, "I was talking to the chief super. He's always got his nose to the ground about these sort of things. Another thing—" He gazed abstractedly out of the window, while Kite waited for him to go on, until Kite realised he wasn't going to.

Kite sat back, feeling squashed but resigned. When Mayo had that look on his face, you'd get nothing but monosyllables out of him until he'd worked out whatever it was that had just occurred to him.

At that moment the owner of the house, Bryan Challis, was driving his silver-grey Jaguar XJ6S aggressively, as he did everything else, back from Mass. His wife Gillian sat in unaccustomed silence beside him.

Penny, their fifteen-year-old daughter, lolled in the back, wishing her mother was driving—she did it ten times better—and debating whether or not to liven things up by saying so. In Penny's opinion, her father needed more practice at driving his own car and more criticism when he did. Turner drove him up to the City each day, while he sat in the back and worked; otherwise, her mother almost always drove. Thinking about it, Penny decided that in the circumstances she'd better not stir things up. Her father might not, as he usually did, simply laugh and call her a precocious brat; Mummy certainly wouldn't. She wouldn't have, even if she'd been in her usual lenient Sunday mood, which she wasn't. You could tell because she wasn't boring on about old Father Flaherty's sermon, and trying to involve the others in debating his arguments, as she invariably did.

In fact, there was a horrid feeling altogether to the weekend. The shock which had come on Friday, via the regional news on TV, had obviously shaken her mother rigid, and cut out everything else as a topic of conversation. Not that they'd talked about it much. After a brief, appalled exchange, when Mummy—Mummy! —had burst into tears and been awkwardly comforted by her father, they'd avoided further discussion, at least in front of her.

Penny could understand, though, how awful it must be for her mother. Fleur Saville had been one of her oldest chums, and one of her do-gooding cronies, as well as being a famous historical novelist. Her parents thought Penny hadn't read the Fleur Lamont books. She had, though, in spite of being forbidden to do so, during the week, when she was away at school, and couldn't see what all the fuss was about. There was worse on TV every night of the week.

As for her father, his mouth had tightened when they'd heard she'd been found dead, but that was all; he sat twisting his black onyx ring, looking solemn, seeming anxious to put the right expression on his face, the way he did when horrifying Third World pictures came on the screen. She knew how he felt. As if it ought to have affected both of them, her father and herself, in the same way as it had Mummy.

There was a car waiting outside the house when the Jag rounded the curve in the drive, right on the spot where her father usually parked. He said a brief forbidden word, then pulled to a stop directly in front of it, sending gravel spurting in all directions.

11

While his wife and daughter went to take off their coats, Challis buttonholed Mayo; they stood facing each other in the centre of an enormous cream-washed, plastered, and beamed hall, large enough to accommodate sundry weighty pieces of black oak furniture and two chintz-covered sofas, as well as several chairs and tables drawn up to a fire that could comfortably have roasted a couple of sheep. Its owner stood with feet planted apart on polished oak boards a foot wide, hands thrust deep into the pockets of his country tweeds. "Look here, I won't have my wife bothered over this affair. She's upset enough as it is."

Mayo's hackles rose, partly at the supercilious "Look here," but more at the man himself, a big, handsome, dark-haired, blue-chinned man of about forty-five, with heavy dark spectacles seeking to underline his air of self-importance. Giving Challis the benefit of his own special brand of cold, grey-eyed stare, he said evenly, "We shan't upset anybody more than we have to, sir, but that's not always avoidable when there's been a murder committed."

"Oh, well, of course, there's no question of being obstructive—" Challis was beginning with a hint of bluster when he was interrupted by the return of his wife.

"Murder?" she repeated. "Murder? They said on the news it was an accident! Oh God." She seemed stunned.

"Perhaps you'd better sit down, ma'am."

"Yes. Oh, yes. And do please take a seat yourselves."

She indicated chairs near the fire with a wave of her hand, sinking into one herself, while Challis said, "If you'll excuse me—er—telephone call to make, you know. You won't want me; I hardly knew her, and I was in Zurich that weekend, didn't get back until late Saturday."

His wife threw him an odd, almost pleading glance, and Mayo resisted the impulse to keep him anyway, just because of his assumption, but in actual fact, his preference was to talk to Gillian Challis alone for the moment, so he let him go. He met Kite's raised eyebrows. Yes, you'd have thought he'd have wanted to stay, if only to give his wife moral support. He hadn't even given her a word of sympathy.

Though very probably she was likely to be less in need of support than most. Evidently to Challis, big was in every way beautiful; his furniture, likewise his wife—though in fact she was not tall, but well-made in a bouncy sort of way, with hips that were beginning to spread. She was almost as fair as Fleur Saville had been, but there the resemblance between the two women ended. Fleur had been slight and pale and slender; Mrs. Challis immediately brought to mind Betjeman's Olympian girl, "standing in strong athletic pose." An attractive woman, she still bore traces of a healthy summer tan, a subtle contrast with her fair hair and blue eyes. She was the daughter of a general and showed it in the speed with which she gathered her forces and regained control and turned her direct gaze on Mayo.

"I'm sorry; it was a shock to hear what you said about Fleur. We heard about it on television, and they didn't say—neither did Edwin—it's really too awful—quite unbelievable! I suppose you've come to see me because I was with her on the day she . . . How can I help you?" She was clearly very upset, but her quick acceptance of the situation was wholly admirable.

Kite took up the questioning at a signal from Mayo, who chose to keep in the background when occasion demanded it, as now, observing witnesses as they answered, or when they were silent. So often what they *didn't* say was more important than what they did.

"I understand she left the hall with you, at about twelve-thirty?" Kite asked.

While admiring the self-control which had taken charge, Mayo noticed Mrs. Challis was not quite as together as she might wish to convey. If she went on fiddling with the winder of that expensive, emerald-set wrist-watch, she'd break it. Everything about her was expensive and well chosen: good suit, shoes that looked handmade, the bag which she'd dropped beside her chair on coming in— square and practical but with heavy gold fittings—yet only the watch shouted it, seeming flashy against the rest of her things.

"It was about half past twelve," she said in answer to Kite's question. "We left the hall together in my car. I was going to drop her at home, but when she said Edwin wouldn't be there for lunch, I suggested we should drive out to the White Boar at Over Kennet and have a ploughman's lunch there, to cheer her up."

"She told you she needed cheering up, did she?"

"Not in so many words, but poor darling, she was having difficulty in breathing, so I knew something was wrong. A lot of her asthma was psychosomatic—you knew she was asthmatic? Yes, well, she used to try not to allow things to get her down because of that." Momentarily, the low, well-modulated voice faltered. "I'm sorry, but I'm not used to the idea yet—she'd always been my closest friend . . . we've known each other ever since we were at school together, she and I."

"And Mrs. Fennimore as well, I believe."

A pause. Mayo thought he detected a slight, very slight drop in temperature. "Oh, yes, Nell too. But of course, almost immediately we left school, Nell got married and started having babies, which meant Fleur and myself were closer than ever. You see, I didn't have Penny until fairly late and Fleur didn't marry early. At one time, it was understood that she and Gerald Fennimore . . . however, we were only eighteen then, and in the end, he chose Nell. Much more suitable choice for a dentist's wife."

Hmm, thought Mayo, as she went on. For a long time, she went on. They had to listen to her on the subject of her friend, on her qualities as a devoted wife, fund raiser, and selfless worker for charity, kind to those who worked for her, loved by her friends: a paragon. "Thank you, darling, put it down there."

This last was to the daughter, Penny, who had come in from the kitchen with coffee which she proceeded to pour; a tall, striking-looking girl of about fifteen, her thick black hair, very like her father's, falling forward over her face as she bent over the four matt chocolate-and-white stoneware coffee cups on the tray. As soon as she'd handed round three of them, her mother said, "Penny, would you be a darling and check up on the lunch?" It was a suggestion made gently, with a smile; nevertheless it brooked no argument.

Her daughter gave her a look which could best be described as old-fashioned, but she picked her own cup and saucer up without demur and went out, back to the kitchen. Presently, she was seen walking past the window with an enormous prancing Airedale-type dog, which bounced along looking deceptively like an oversize stuffed toy. Mayo didn't like Airedales; they were a disagreeable sort of dog that would have your arm for lunch as soon as look at you.

"Mrs. Challis," Kite was beginning again after this interlude, "we can assume Mrs. Saville would tell you why she was depressed, seeing you were such good friends?"

She took a sip of her black sugarless coffee and said carefully, "In the end she did. She admitted she'd had a quarrel with Edwin, which had upset her dreadfully. She didn't tell me what it was about, and I didn't ask, but it couldn't have been anything trivial; neither of them was at all that sort of person."

"So what time did you leave the White Boar?"

"About ten past one."

"And it's about a ten-minute drive back into Lavenstock—"

"Oh, but we didn't go straight back. It was very stuffy in the pub, and she asked me to drive somewhere so she could get a breath of air. She wanted to get back to Lavenstock for a hair appointment she'd made at that new shop just round the corner from the church hall, but we'd plenty of time, so we drove back slowly by way of Kennet Edge. It's usually very bracing up there, but that day it was sleeting and altogether not very pleasant, so we didn't get out of the car after all. Anyway, time was getting on by then, and she seemed anxious to be off. She'd never been to this hairdresser previously, and she didn't want to be late, though *why* she wanted to go there one can't imagine. Not our sort of place. More—well, for younger people, at any rate. When I said so, she said maybe it was time she changed her image before—before it was too late." Her voice shook a little on the last words, and she paused, looking down at her large, capable hands, but when she resumed her voice was firm again. "It did occur to me, with her saying that, that maybe the quarrel with Edwin had been over another woman, a younger woman perhaps—but only for a moment. If Fleur suspected that, she was very much mistaken."

"What time was this appointment, Mrs. Challis?" Kite asked.

"Quarter to two. I stopped at the corner of Peter Street to let her get out, just before the appointment was due, only for a moment—you know what the traffic's like on that corner—and that . . . was the last time I saw her, her red coat disappearing into the shop."

"After you'd left her, did you go straight back to the Church Hall?"

"Me? Oh, no, I parked my car round the back of the hall, then did a bit of shopping. I only wanted one or two bits, but everywhere was so busy, I only just got back in time."

"What did you think when Mrs. Saville never turned up?"

"Frankly, I was astonished, but when I heard later from Mrs. Fennimore she'd gone to the cottage, I assumed she'd taken herself off to—well, teach Edwin a lesson, or something. She was, you know, sometimes given to rather extravagant gestures."

Kite had come to the end of his questions and looked at Mayo for help. Mayo said, "Mrs. Challis, did you know Mr. Saville's first wife?"

"Margaret?" She turned towards him, giving him a long, level look, unsurprised at the change of direction. "Yes, though I knew her younger sister Kathleen better. I say *knew* because she—Kathleen, that is—went out to South Africa after the accident. She was dreadfully cut up about Margaret dying, and all the unpleasantness that followed."

"The first Mrs. Saville died in an accident?"

"Didn't you know? They were on a sailing holiday and she was drowned. Edwin was quite devastated, left alone with a young son to bring up. I think that's partly why he married Fleur so quickly."

"What actually happened?"

"I don't sail, and I never understood exactly what it was—something to do with her head being struck with the boom. She fell overboard and was drowned. Edwin wasn't a very experienced sailor, the weather was rough, and the coroner had some very cogent things to say about irresponsibility." She checked a sharp sigh, changing it to a nod of approval. It was the sort of attitude she publicly supported. "He was quite right, of course, and I suppose Edwin deserved a certain amount of criticism. All the same," she went on, strongly, in the voice familiar in the magistrates' court, "I'd like you to understand that there could have been no question—no question at all—of it being anything other than an accident."

"Was it ever suggested it wasn't?"

"There were unkind things said; there often are when money is involved, and Margaret left a good deal. It was put about that perhaps her death had been—fortuitous. Which was absolutely ridiculous, of course."

"You seem very certain, Mrs. Challis."

"Of course I am. Because I've known Edwin Saville for many years, and I know him utterly incapable of violence; it's quite out of character." As if that clinched the matter, she checked the time rather obviously on her watch.

"We won't keep you much longer, but I'd like to ask you a little more about the relationship between Mrs. Saville and her husband. You thought it unlikely in her husband's case that there was any other—friend?" Mayo despised himself for the euphemism, but Mrs. Challis had that effect on him. "What about Mrs. Saville?"

She immediately grew cold. "Certainly not. No question of it, on either side." She sounded, like Jennifer Pound, as though sex was confined to the lower classes. "I can't think why I mentioned it." Neither, for that matter, could Mayo.

"Thank you, then; I think that'll do for the present, Mrs. Challis." He'd lost her now, anyway. "You've been very helpful. In the meantime, if there's anything else you think of, perhaps you'd let us know?"

"Of course." She relented. "I'm only sorry I haven't been able to help you more now. It's been such a shock. One can't—one can't imagine life without Fleur." She looked suddenly quite wretched.

Kite took it on himself to say, "Don't worry, Mrs. Challis, we'll get whoever did it, in the end."

Her low-voiced answer was unexpected, and not only because people didn't say things like that anymore. "Yes, well, have charity. Let's not forget that whoever did this is a soul in torment."

Kite looked as if the floor opening under his feet would be a happy alternative to having to find an answer to that one, and even Mayo, not easily outfaced, was momentarily taken aback. Though not necessarily agreeing with her, he mentally gave himself a black mark for insensitivity; he had never suspected that beneath that unwavering sense of justice there lurked compassion.

Bryan Challis stood at his study window and watched the car with the two policemen disappear down the long sweep of the drive, a worried man.

He was making mistakes these days, too many. He'd very nearly said more than he ought. He'd told a useless lie, one which the police could easily disprove. Too late he saw that; but it had never been in his mind that they would have cause to question him, and nor had they, he reflected, relaxing visibly at the realisation. He'd nothing to worry about. After all, what was there to connect him with Fleur Saville, to arouse suspicions?

He lit a cigarette and poured himself a stiff malt whisky—the best he had handy, Laphroaig, an indulgence he felt he deserved.

Where had it all begun, the chain of cause and effect, his involvement with these women?

With Fleur? With Gillian? Or Ruth? With Candace Neale, a name from the grave after all these years? Or with his own Catholic upbringing, guilt never far from the surface, sins unconfessed and retribution ever hanging by a thread over his head?

He wore his religion more lightly than Gillian could ever wear hers; nevertheless, the sense of sin was never too far away—to be reasoned with, rationalised, excused, but never completely exorcised. It had been behind the driving ambition which had enabled him to offer Gillian a lifestyle which only he knew was an atonement.

These were thoughts not usually present in his mind. Normally, he did not allow them to surface; they were present only as a subterranean undercurrent to his life, a dark tide that could only be endured by ignoring it. Or when that was impossible, by lavishing upon his wife and daughter expensive presents . . . the luxury cruise down the Nile, the white Audi Quattro with personalised number-plates, the new pony, and this Christmas the emerald-set watch. They said emeralds were unlucky . . .

Sometimes, when he had caught her eye resting speculatively upon him or sensed a refusal to meet his gaze, he had wondered, with a plunge of something like fear; when she had opened the Cartier box on Christmas morning, for instance, he had caught an unprecedented glint of tears in her eyes. He had told himself it was an understandable reaction when someone was touched by an overwhelmingly extravagant gesture of affection. It couldn't possibly be that she knew, or even suspected. Gillian was incapable of that sort of complicity in her marriage.

12

"You have to admit it smells to high heaven—two wives dying in suspicious circumstances, both leaving him money."

Kite's sentiment was one with which Mayo was, rationally, bound to agree. Yet without proof, where were they? All the evidence against Saville so far was circumstantial. Moreover, since the talk with Gillian Challis, the margins had narrowed considerably. There was now, taking into consideration the findings of the post-mortem, not much more than half an hour or so after having had her hair done during which Fleur Saville could have been killed. During which time, from two-thirty to three, there were apparently unassailable witnesses to swear that Edwin Saville had been serving in his shop.

They'd been trying to fit in these newest facts with what they already knew for the last fifteen minutes, over a tough roast beef sandwich at an unprepossessing and almost deserted roadside pub on the way back to Lavenstock, where they'd arranged to meet the editor of the *Advertiser*, and Kite was looking gloomy, perhaps because of the flatness of the beer, perhaps at seeing his favourite suspect being ruled out. "It's always within the bounds of possibility that one or other of 'em, the witnesses, might discover they've been mistaken about the times," he pressed on, hopefully.

Mayo shook his head. It was possible, yes, but probable? He didn't think so. He didn't think Kite did either, by now, although he wasn't about to give up. "He's the best bet we've got—the *only* bet—including this hypothetical lover . . . and it'll surprise me if we find Waterton *hasn't* spent the last month chasing elephants with a camera."

Mayo looked at his watch. Sutcliffe was late.

"Okay—supposing, just for the sake of argument, she changed

her mind at the last minute. Mrs. Challis saw her disappearing
through the door of that hair-dressing place, but she could have
walked out again. Supposing she went along to Butter Lane instead, and Saville killed her there. That's why he didn't answer the
door to Mrs. Wilson."

"And went on serving his customers as though nothing had happened? Well, all right, yes, as far as Saville's concerned, I'd go along
with that. If anybody could do it, he could." Kite looked interested,
then frowned.

"What's on your mind, Martin? Apart from the origins of this
so-called beef? Chased many a man up a tree before it got into this
sandwich, I reckon." Mayo removed a piece of gristle from his
mouth and abandoned the rest of his lunch.

"I've just remembered something Gerald Fennimore said. He
took his dog for a walk down to the park that afternoon . . ."

"And?"

"The quickest way from his house is via the backs of the houses
along Kelsey Road. It cuts quite a corner off, and you can let your
dog off the lead there."

"Right." He remembered the fat, bossy corgi and its owner. "Go
on."

"It's a long shot, I suppose—but didn't Mrs. Challis say there'd
been something between Mrs. Saville and Fennimore once? You
don't think it's possible he's been carrying a torch for her all these
years?"

Mayo considered. It *was* a long shot. "I don't see it. Or that he
nipped in and did for her while taking his dog for a walk. Not
without any other suspicion. Might as well suspect *Mrs.* Fennimore. We'll bear it in mind, but we're not so desperate yet."

All the same, the photograph Nell Fennimore had given him,
with Gerald in evening clothes, the matinee-idol image, came to
mind. But dammit, you couldn't start suspecting a man of murder
just because he looked like an out-of-date film star. He looked up as
the door opened. "Here's Sutcliffe."

"So you want to know about Fleur? Yes, of course I remember
her. She worked for us at the *Advertiser* ever since she left school at

eighteen—right up until she married Saville, in fact." Jim Sutcliffe, the editor of the *Lavenstock Advertiser*, was a short, talkative man with gingery whiskers, a small round pot-belly, a permanent cigarette in his mouth, and a resident cough. He was due to retire shortly—if the cough hadn't carried him off before then.

"Was she writing then—those books of hers, I mean?" Mayo asked.

"No, I don't think so—well, I know she wasn't, because I've always taken credit for starting her off on that lark. When she left to marry Saville, she said to me, 'Well, Jim, that's the end of my career; he doesn't approve of women going out to work.' She was laughing when she said it, though; she knew when she was on to a good thing. Saville wasn't short then, not at that time, not with all his first wife had left him. Anyway, I suggested she tried writing fiction to keep her occupied—'after all,' I said, 'you've been doing it for years, haven't you, dear?'"

"What did you mean by that?"

"Oh, it was just a joke." Sutcliffe looked a bit uncomfortable and buried his face in his glass. He drank nothing but draught Guiness and was already well down his second half. "If she thought a story wasn't interesting enough, she'd embroider it, and it used to get my goat. It's all right bringing tears to your readers' eyes occasionally by laying it on, but there's a limit. We had no end of set-to's about it. Trouble was, life was never exciting enough for her—she had to dramatise it."

"Why d'you think she stayed in Lavenstock then? You'd have thought she'd have gone for the big city and the bright lights," Kite said.

Sutcliffe drew on his cigarette and coughed, hollowly. "Funny thing about Fleur. She used to talk enough about getting out, but she never did it; basically she was a small-town girl, bourgeoise, as they say, by upbringing and inclination. She was pretty tough behind all that feminine veneer, realistic enough anyway to know that she'd hate it like hell being a very small fish in a big, big pond. Suited her down to the ground it did, being the famous author, getting the kudos for all those fund-raising efforts, acting the Queen Bee with her retinue behind her."

"Sycophants?" Mayo, watching the rapidity with which the Guiness level was going down, made a sign to Kite, who went to the bar to get another round in.

"Some of them, yes. But they seemed to stay around, most of them, so it must have been a bit more than that."

"What about men?"

"She had one or two skirmishes before she met Saville, but it wasn't men turned her on."

"What then? Women?"

"God, no, not in that way." Sutcliffe drank up and sucked the froth from his moustache, giving the question some thought before answering more fully. "Power, of a sort," he said at last. "At least, she liked to see people dancing on the end of her string, no doubt about that. It's a kind of aphrodisiac in its way. Thanks, Martin. Cheers."

Kite resumed his seat and Mayo said, "What d'you know about the accident to Saville's first wife, Jim?"

"Margaret? Oh, you're going back a bit now." The journalist eyed Mayo speculatively. "It *was* just an accident, take it from me. There was a lot of talk, which I take it you know about, but there was nothing in it. As far as I can see, the whole thing was caused simply through lack of nous. Sailing by unqualified amateurs should be banned. And Saville's a bit simple, you know, like a lot more so-called intelligent people. He might have got a first at Cambridge, but he doesn't know his arse from his elbow. I'd be willing to bet, though I've nothing to base this on, that there isn't a penny of Margaret's money left. That shop of his could be a little gold mine if he went about it the right way, but he's no idea; half the time it's not open when you want to pop in—he's off at some bloody sale or other. If you ask him to get you a book, he forgets to order it; the shop's only there for his own interest."

Half of this Mayo agreed with; about the other half he wasn't so sure. Saville was layers deeper than Sutcliffe was giving him credit for. All this surface incompetence—Mayo was more than ready to believe it might well be an act, put on by a basically lazy man to save himself from the necessity of stirring himself to action.

"Tell you another thing about Fleur—you never knew when you

had her, that one. Always something up her sleeve. Always looked as if she knew summat you didn't—know what I mean?"

Mayo did. That photograph again, that closed Giaconda smile. Was it something she had known or done that had caused someone to murder her?

Sutcliffe lit the last cigarette from his packet and looked at his watch. "Look, I don't want to rush you, but if there's nothing else you want to know, I'd best be off. Vera'll give me hell if I ruin her Yorkshire pudding."

There wasn't at the moment, except for what Sutcliffe might know about Michael Saville, or Zoe Henderson, but Mayo drew a blank here. There was nothing the journalist could tell about either of them. Not one to hang about, he accepted their thanks and left, happy with a promise to be kept informed of anything further on the case of interest to his paper, and another forty fags bought at the bar.

Coming into Lavenstock from the direction of Branxmore, dominating the landscape were the tall shoddy tower blocks of the Somerville Estate, a nineteen-sixties civic mistake that strode aggressively against the skyline, as if about to stamp forward and crush the parade of small, depressed shops at their feet. The shops today were all shut, with the exception of Patel's Punjabi Supermarket; their motto was "We never close." Outside the fish-and-chip shop, greasy wrappers lay discarded and sodden in the gutters, yesterday's frying still lingering on the thick, damply cold air.

They drew up outside Elizabeth House, a block of maisonettes, newer than the towers, built in their shadow, and walked to the door of Number Twenty.

"Oy oy!" Kite bent down to make a closer inspection of about two thousand pounds' worth of a powerful motor bike, casually propped against the wall. "Did you say on the dole?" The door was at that moment opened, before they'd had time to knock, by Lola Tennyson, a quick, darting figure, her raggedy-blond hair newly rinsed.

"You've found her, haven't you? Mrs. Saville?" were the first words she uttered, almost before Mayo had got the introductions out of his mouth. Her clothes, he saw at once, were too young and too bright, defeating the presumed object of making her look younger than her years, her expression too eager and too avid. Mayo indicated that they had, and they followed her from the tiny hallway into the living room, where a young girl of about seventeen or so was curled up in one of the armchairs, giving the impression of having hurriedly pushed something under the cushion as they came in. The room was warm and comfortable, and tidy, very tidy considering that there were three teenagers in the household, and apart from a blindingly patterned carpet in shades of orange and gold, plainly furnished, with a three-piece suite in mustard-coloured vinyl at one end and a light wood dining suite at the other. Heavy rock music reverberated through the floor from upstairs.

"Mr. Saville rang my Debra here to tell her," her mother went on, projecting her voice above the racket. "She used to do Mrs. Saville's typing and things like that for her, see, and he rang to say there wouldn't be no more work. What a terrible thing—she's been working for her for over two years now, haven't you m'duck?" It was unclear whether Mrs. Tennyson's outrage was for Fleur Saville's death or her own daughter's unemployment.

Debra rose abruptly and made as if to go out of the room. "Would you mind staying, please?" Mayo asked. She looked apprehensive, but sat down again without saying anything. She was a surprise, this Debra, a thin, grave girl, dressed in a white T-shirt and jeans, with a mass of dark hair, untidily crimped as they all seemed to wear it nowadays, and brown eyes which were wide and thoughtful behind a pair of large spectacles.

"Sorry about the noise," their hostess apologised perfunctorily, "it's our Kev," as though that was both explanation and excuse. They were just in time for a cuppa, she added, she'd just brewed up, and she was sorry, but our Kev had eaten all the biscuits. Tea would do fine, Mayo said; they'd stopped for a bite of lunch on the way there.

When they'd accepted cups of the fierce orange brew, and Kite had settled back, notebook at the ready, Mayo said, "I'd like to ask you one or two questions, Mrs. Tennyson." She wasn't Mrs.—that much he knew; also that she never bothered to conceal it—but what else did you call a woman in her position? His mind and his tongue jibbed at Ms.

"I heard them, you know, her and him, the day she disappeared, having a right old go at one another. Poor man, he must be feeling really bad now, knowing they parted in anger!" The kind of eagerness in the way she came out with the cliché was something Mayo wasn't unfamiliar with, in circumstances like this. He leaned forward to place his cup on the coffee table and rephrased the first part of her remark.

"I understand you overheard what you thought was a quarrel on that day."

"I didn't *think* I heard; I *did* hear."

She was agog to tell, repeating what she'd heard, but despite her claims, there was nothing that was new. What it amounted to in total was raised voices and an assumption of the rest. Nothing had been clearly enough heard for her to be able to tell him what the quarrel had been about, she was forced to admit, but never in her life had she expected to hear Mr. Saville shout like that; a real saint that man was, the way Mrs. Saville only had to raise her little finger and he'd do what she wanted. "And now she's ended up murdered, hasn't she?"

"We don't know that." He wasn't prepared to tell her yet that they did.

"Murdered," she repeated with relish, as if he hadn't spoken, "Mrs. Saville, fancy!"

"Mum!" interposed the hitherto silent Debra.

"Mrs. Tennyson, we're trying to sort out the events on that Saturday. Mr. Saville tells us that he spoke to you in the Cornmarket late in the afternoon, is that right?"

"That's right, he did."

"I don't suppose you could give me a more precise time?"

It appeared she could. "A minute or two after half-four, it'd be. The town hall clock had just struck when we started collecting. I told him about forgetting my money and he gave it me, and more for the box, very generous, I'll hand that to him—"

"Just a minute. What money was this?" Saville had made no mention of this part of his encounter with Lola.

"The extra that Mrs. Saville had given me for going in that day to help out. Forgot it, I did, left it on the kitchen table, being in such a rush. I had to go up the town to do some Christmas shopping after I'd finished my work, and I got a real turn, I can tell you, when I found I'd forgotten to pick it up. In Marks I was. I had enough with me, but I never like the idea of money being left lying around; it don't come that easy."

"That is doesn't." Mayo gave her one of his sudden rare smiles, getting a never-say-die grin back in return. Life must be far from a bed of roses for her, but she was a little game 'un, right enough, and she didn't seem to be making a bad job of it. He'd seen more than his share of women like her, left on their own to keep the family going on tuppence ha'penny a week. Marvellous how they did it—but then, he'd known for a long time that women were by far the tougher section of the human race. Her courage moved him. He reckoned she was entitled to her Salvation Army if it gave her a kick. "Please go on."

"Well, she'd put it in an old envelope, see, and I thought what if it gets thrown away? But I knew it wasn't no use calling nor ringing to find out; there wouldn't be nobody there—Mr. Saville would be at the shop, and Mrs. Saville was at the kiddies' party. I didn't half get a surprise when I saw his car outside when I was going home on the bus."

"Whose car?"

"Mr. Saville's, of course."

"What time was this?"

Her eyes widened at the rapid questions. "My bus was the twenty to three from outside the library, and it was on time for a change, so that would make it, let's see, about what, when it got to Kelsey Road—?"

"Quarter to, no more than ten to at the most," Kite supplied, unable to keep a note of excitement from his voice.

"That's right, it would." Gratified by the interest she'd aroused, Lola settled back in her chair, curling sparrow legs under her, the tip of her snub nose turning pink with all the attention she was getting. "So I rang straight away when I got home—that'd be about another fifteen minutes, I reckon—and there was this feller answered. I thought it was Mr. Saville, but he said it wasn't."

"What made you think it was him?" Mayo asked.

"I was expecting him to answer, I suppose," she responded with a shrewdly assessing glance. "But when he said it wasn't, I could tell the difference, really. Quicker, more impatient like. 'No, there's nobody here who can help you, sorry,' he said, sharpish, and put the receiver down. Well, I thought, some folk!"

If Saville had just killed his wife, it would be surprising if he hadn't sounded strange. But he couldn't have, could he?

"You're sure it was Mr. Saville's car you saw?"

"Yes, of course. Leastways, if it wasn't, it was one just like it. I've seen it often enough, haven't I? Sort of grey-blue it is."

"What kind is it, what make?" Kite wanted to know.

"How should I know? I'm not well up on cars; I've never had no cause to be. But it must have been his, mustn't it?"

The thumping beat from upstairs ceased suddenly. It was followed by a loud crash, as if Kev had thrown his boot, or perhaps his stereo, against the wall. Then the music began again, louder. His mum said, "Ooh, our Kev! We'll have her next door banging on the wall again before we know where we're at! Hang on, will you?" and rushed out.

Mayo seized the opportunity, which he suspected would be brief, to speak to Debra. "So you'll be looking for a new job now, love?"

"Yes, I suppose so." To his surprise Mayo heard a catch in the girl's voice as she answered. Well, it wasn't easy nowadays for any of them, poor kids. It wasn't easy to give them reassurance, either.

"A bright girl like you, you'll find something," he told her, doing his best.

"No, I shan't. Not another job like that. Working for her was special. Like—" Tears welled, one rolled down her face. "Oh, I don't know how I can find words to describe how it was," she finished forlornly, looking young and lost.

"Try, Debra."

She blew her nose and tried.

Her lip still trembled, but gradually as she began to speak, she became calmer. It turned out that she'd acted as the dead woman's secretary for getting on for three years. She hadn't been able to find work for several months after leaving school, and she'd been glad to accept the job Fleur had offered. "I could hardly type at all when I started, never mind type manuscripts, but it was a job. That's all I thought of it at first, but in the end I got to really love it, you know? Besides—" Whatever she had been about to say, she checked herself, blinking rapidly. Her hand strayed towards the cushion and whatever she had stuffed behind it.

"You mean the job was well paid?"

"Oh, no! Well, it was all right, but . . . she was good to me in other ways."

She looked at him earnestly, stole a glance at Kite, apparently absorbed in his shorthand, and then in a burst of confidence, she told him shyly, colouring up, "I've been trying to do a bit of writing, myself. Mum thinks it's daft, somebody like me hoping to get anything published, and if our Kev knew . . . but why not?" she added defiantly.

"Why not?" said Mayo, concealing his surprise. "Good luck to you, lass." He was rewarded with a smile that seemed to light the grave face from within, giving it a sheen of beauty, making him blink and feel a pang of middle-aged envy for such shining youth, such hope. "What about Mrs. Saville, did she know about your writing?"

"Oh, yes!" breathed Debra. "Of course, I know I can't ever hope to write as well as she did, but she used to read my stuff and tell me I was learning all the time, show me where I'd gone wrong." She added modestly, "Working for her like I did, I don't suppose I could help some of it rubbing off, could I?"

A bad case of heroine worship, no doubt about it, but not perhaps entirely unjustified. A busy woman, taking time off to help an inexperienced young girl on her way—that had been a kindness. And if Fleur Saville had exacted a bit of flattery and admiration in the course of it, wasn't that only human? She had liked both, though perhaps more than most, he thought, recalling what Zoe

Henderson had said about her—confirmed by Sutcliffe, and also, according to Kite, by the vicar's wife.

"There's something I'd like to ask you—" Debra was saying, her face vivid with colour, stammering in her confusion. "I don't—I don't know if it's allowed—but if you—if you do come across it. It's, well—it's a manuscript of mine, you see. Could I p-possibly have it back?"

"I should think so, if you tell me what to look for."

"Well, I've written a book," she said, her voice steadying, chin raised, her expression a mixture of pride and defiance, as if daring him to laugh. She threw another glance at Kite but seemed reassured. "I didn't think it could be much good, but Mrs. Saville thought it was worth sending to her publisher. Only, the thing is, she rang me that morning—the morning she disappeared—and told me she'd had it back. They'd written to her, and there were some comments in the letter about my script. They don't want to publish my story, of course—I never expected that—but she said they'd been kind about it, so—if I could have it? My book, I mean; I expect you'll want to keep the letter, and it—it d-doesn't really matter very much to me."

She was painfully anxious not to seem anxious about what must be of the greatest importance to her. "Deborah Shelley?" he asked, rapidly making the thinly disguised connection. He recalled seeing the letter she was talking about amongst the dead woman's papers, and he particularly remembered the section in it that had referred to the book. If he'd been an aspiring author, he'd thought, he'd have been greatly encouraged by the remarks.

"You've seen it! Oh, you haven't—?" Her face suddenly paled. "You haven't *read* it?"

Not the book, he told her gently, only the letter. He had just time to add that he would let her have her manuscript back and a photocopy of the criticism when he heard her mother's hand on the doorknob. He jerked his head in Kite's direction. Kite got up and walked unhurriedly to the door. Voices could be heard— Kite's, Lola's shrill tones, and then presently, the sound of heavier footsteps descending the stairs.

"Debra," Mayo said quickly, "you probably knew as much about

Mrs. Saville's affairs as anybody. Do you recall anything different that happened lately? Had she changed her routine, made any new contacts?" Debra shook her head, mystified. "Anything at all out of the ordinary that you remember?"

"No, nothing like that, except—" She broke off, looking thoughtful. "No, it's too long ago, and nothing ever came of it."

"Tell me, all the same."

"Well, it wasn't recently; it was months ago, after she'd been up to London to see her publishers. They're being taken over by an American firm, and when she came back, I could see something exciting had happened. She'd met one of the American executives, and when she came home, she was all sort of lit up. I knew there'd been some talk a while back about televising *Salamander Fire* as a serial, and I asked her if that was it. But she laughed and said something more rewarding and important than that."

"She didn't explain any further?"

"No, never another word."

"I don't suppose you'd remember the date?"

Debra only had to think for a second or two. "Oh, yes, I can tell you exactly. July the third it would be. I can remember because it was my birthday the following week, and when she was in London, she bought me this." She lovingly touched the gold chain around her neck, from which hung an elegant gold letter *D*. "But it was funny, her saying that, wasn't it? I mean, what could be more important than a TV serial?"

"What indeed?" replied Mayo.

"That your lad's motor-bike?" he asked a minute later, finding Mrs. Tennyson and Kite outside with a sullen youth sporting a bright green Mohican haircut and several diamanté earrings dangling from three perforations in one ear.

"That's what he's been on to me about, and yes, it is, and what of it?" Lola demanded militantly, jerking her head towards Kite. "He's just got a job up the motorway construction site—nearly two hundred a week he's earning, so why shouldn't he buy a motorbike if he wants?"

"All right, love, keep your hair on," Kite answered. "No harm in asking." And to Kev, "Let's have a dekko at your licence and insurance all the same, sunshine."

Two hundred a week, for a layabout like that, a bit of a kid who'd left school without an O level to his name and a record to boot? I should be so lucky, he thought, reflecting on a policeman's lot.

13

As usual, there had been an instant response to the appeal on radio and TV for anyone who might have seen Fleur Saville on the day she disappeared. Back at the office, Mayo found on his desk a whole clutch of reports that she'd been sighted. A woman answering to her description had bought petrol at a filling station near Cheltenham and driven away in a black Volvo (but Fleur Saville didn't drive). She'd been seen at Euston station at eleven (the time when she'd been putting out cakes and sandwiches in the Church Hall in Lavenstock), also in Birmingham, in Stratford-upon-Avon, and in Lossiemouth, four hundred miles away in Scotland. There were more. They'd all have to be taken note of and the possibles investigated.

Meanwhile, he'd better have another look at the dead woman's papers, after what young Debra had said. He rang for some tea and drank it while he went through them yet again. It didn't take him long to find the publishers' letter she'd spoken about, dated the sixteenth of December, which he put on one side in order to photocopy for her the section concerning her manuscript. He then went backwards through the file until he came across the carbon copy of a letter Fleur had written to them, after the London meeting on the third of July. It said thank you for the excellent lunch and spoke of "the matters we discussed" without specifying what these had been. It went on to say how unexpected it was to find they had mutual friends; she was sure they'd all find it very interesting to meet again here in Lavenstock, and ended "Very sincerely, Fleur Lamont."

Mayo noted the name of the person to whom the letter was addressed, and sat back, thinking deeply.

Fleur had learned something that day which had, in Debra's

phrase, lit her up. It didn't necessarily have to be anything which had occurred at her publishers', or course, but it seemed likely.

Or what other things were capable of exciting Fleur? Being centre stage . . . she was quick to seize upon the drama of a situation, and the opportunity of basking in the limelight seemed never to have been far from her mind. She had liked power. Manipulating someone to her advantage.

He looked again at the letter. Was he imagining the veiled threat that seemed contained in that last brief paragraph? He allowed his mind to dwell on the subject of it: a mutual acquaintance—something more interesting, apparently, even than televising *Salamander Fire*. He closed his eyes, trying to remember exactly what she'd said to Debra. *"Oh no, something much more interesting than that."* No, he hadn't quite got it . . . *"something more interesting and rewarding."* Had that been the precise word Fleur had used? *Rewarding?*

He decided to search the Buttercup Club files yet again. The idea that had come to him while waiting outside the Challis house was growing in his mind. It wasn't very clear yet, but if he didn't pursue it, he knew he'd get no peace.

It was just before half past seven when Mayo finally put his key into the door of his flat. As soon as he let himself in, it hit him. Although not an unduly gregarious man, he would never have remained solitary through choice, and the bleak loneliness overwhelmed him with the feeling that his life had fallen apart, a sense of personal failure. Depression like this didn't come so often now, but it was still hard to take, and it always came when he wasn't prepared for it . . . after an unrewarding day, in a crowded room, coming unexpectedly on something that had belonged to Lynne . . .

He'd worked out his routines to combat it. Doggedly, now, he brought them into play, upping the thermostat of the central heating, then taking a shower. Later, in his dressing gown, he began to potter about until he should feel like getting himself something to eat. A beer, some Dvořák going, vigorous rhythms suggesting strong forward movement and controlled energy which rarely failed to help him sooner or later to shrug off his mood.

He tried to settle down with the Sunday papers, and his book, but the papers were too full of the usual post-Christmas features on glamorous holidays in far-flung places, and Henry James's Maisie suddenly seemed a tiresome, precocious little perisher who knew too much and whose neck he could cheerfully have wrung. The TV offered nothing but a soap opera about sailing, and a comedy show repeat which hadn't amused him the first time round. The appeal of *Salamander Fire* was nil. On an impulse he fetched out the clock he had mentioned to Zoe Henderson. Tinkering with some form of machinery, preferably a clock or a watch, had always been a form of mind release for him. There was something soothing about letting his hands perform the mechanistic exercise of cleaning and oiling the beautifully machined springs and wheels, fitting them together again in their interdependent, logical pattern, shifting his mind onto automatic pilot.

A small Edwardian bracket clock this was, about six inches high, a pretty thing veneered in walnut, inlaid with ebony, with only a small part of the veneer missing, a corner of the base. That wasn't why it had been put to the back of the cupboard, but because it had stopped at ten to four and refused to go again, and he couldn't abide a clock that wasn't in working order. They spoke too eloquently of empty houses, lives that had stopped. He began to fiddle with it, and before he knew where he was, he had the parts spread out over the table.

The idea that had come to him had been sparked off by something that had been said during the course of the day, and it was frustrating him because he couldn't remember what it was. Usually when this happened, he ignored it, knowing that it was likely to come back to him when he least expected it, when it might or might not turn out to be of importance. But tonight it nagged, as if it were the missing key piece in a Chinese puzzle that he must find. He hated unanswered questions; he liked things to fit into a pattern; perhaps that's why he'd become a detective, trying to replace unrelated parts into his own idea of an ordered scheme of things, though Lynne used to tease him, saying it was because he was just a Nosey Parker, with a talent for sniffing things out that people would often rather have kept hidden. That had been at the beginning of their marriage, when the inconvenient demands of his job could still be made light of with a joke.

Hell, this was getting him nowhere. What was all this with Lynne tonight? She was gone; nothing would bring her back, unsay the things that had been said and not said; nothing could tidy up and smooth out the past.

He reassembled the clock, setting it down carefully and watching it for a while. The music stopped and he went to start the record again from the beginning. The clock went on ticking, quietly, steadily, and he sat back, pleased at last with his efforts. Was it something Mrs. Tennyson had said, or perhaps the girl Debra? Or was it simply that unexpected remark of Gillian Challis's, "Have charity" that had lodged in his head because of its unexpectedness? No, not that, but—

The door bell rang.

It was Alex, with a brown paper carrier bag in her hands. "All right if I come in, Gil? I know it's late, but—"

"All *right?* You can't know how all right it is." But he had a moment of dismay. No way would Alex fail to notice the untidiness of the flat. Very particular, she was. He kept it clean enough, but the niceties of plumped-up cushions and fresh flowers and washing up his breakfast coffee cup every time before he went out was something he just couldn't be bothered with . . . he hoped she wouldn't insist on washing up before she sat down, as she had the last time.

But there was a smile in her eyes; the cold air had brought a flare of colour to her pale cheeks; she looked luminously pretty in a softly wrapped mole-coloured tweed coat with the collar turned up to frame her face and a Gitane-blue scarf that echoed the blue of her eyes tucked in at the neck. He drew her inside, circling her lightly with his arms.

"You've not eaten?" she asked. "Good. Just put this in the oven then, to keep hot; put the plates in, too. It's only Chinese takeaway, not one of your Julie's *cordon bleu* efforts, but I'd been to the pictures and saw your light on as I passed and decided to take a chance."

That sounded like a lonely Sunday evening, a clutch at his heart, but he knew he was on shaky ground, saying a thing like that to Alex. Don't push your luck, when she's doing the running. "I'll just clear the table," he said instead.

Her glance followed the wave of his hand. "Another clock!"

"What d'you mean, another?"

"How many is it? Six, at least. In a flat this size?"

"Seven, actually." He laughed at her expression. "Runs in the family, you should see the number my father had. He used to fiddle with them, as well, till his eyesight got too bad; so did my grandad. I'd forgotten what good therapy it is, even if you don't get it right the first time." He stared at the clock, frowning. It had stopped again. "Give me a minute and I'll have it all away."

"Don't bother, we'll have it on trays, by the fire—and leave the music on, as well."

"Sure you don't object?"

"Love it."

Dvořák's seventh symphony swept gloriously through the room with great melodic surges while they ate. His tiredness had left him. This was how it could be, he thought, not just occasionally, but every night, if they were married. How many times had he asked her? How many times had she put him off—they were all right as they were, weren't they? Why spoil things? *Spoil?* He couldn't understand her and was beginning to feel he was entitled to demand more explanation than that, but he was more afraid than he liked to admit that if he did he might lose her altogether.

He awoke, as he always did, at the dawn light, but Alex was awake before him. And up, out of bed, even dressed, sitting by the window where the curtain had been left half drawn. The view outside was worth looking at, a still, predominantly white landscape with a necklace of lights stringing the road down the tree-lined hill, sweeping in a curve round the edges of the town, to a glimpse of the Stockwell and the hills rising behind. Not enticing enough though, in his opinion, to bring you out of a warm bed on a winter's morning. He lay, lazily content, enjoying watching her without her knowledge, curled up and self-contained in the old rose-patterned chintz armchair. He could see her profile, darker against the still dark sky, her smoothed hair re-forming the memory of it rumpled on his pillow.

She turned slightly when after a while he got out of bed, threw on his bathrobe, and padded over to her to put his arms around her, crossing them over her breasts, deciding that now was the time, now, in the aftermath of love, when things could be spoken about.

Alex too was aware that her time of procrastination was over as, stricken with guilt, she listened to his low murmur, but didn't hear, didn't need to hear, knowing what he was saying by heart . . .

"Don't, Gil," she found courage to interrupt at last, sharper than she meant to, sharp as icicles it came out, so that there was no mistaking either tone or meaning. "It's no good."

He was immediately silent, and for so long she thought he wasn't going to reply. "That's it, then?" he said at last, drawing away. "No good? And here was I thinking it was. Bloody good. Bloody marvellous, in fact."

They were facing each other now.

"I didn't mean *that*. You know I didn't. It was lovely, but, oh God—there's no way I can marry you."

"I see. Good enough in bed, but you can't stand my table manners—"

"Don't blow it up, just listen, won't you? There's a lot I haven't told you."

"You'd better start then, hadn't you?"

It wasn't going to be easy, but then, she'd never thought it would be. He listened, stony-faced, while she told him at last. At last. About her Irish Liam, her dark Celtic charmer with the golden tongue, married to an invalid wife, with no intention of divorcing her. "Not that I'd want him to—I wouldn't want him under those conditions," she said, though for years she'd had him under worse conditions than that. Until at last she'd had enough of subterfuge, of not belonging, of feeling herself used, and had made the break and had herself transferred here.

And nothing had changed, because she'd brought herself with her, and she was still the same. Telling yourself you could *make* it be all right didn't work, as last night had proved. Lying awake, it had come to her like a tremendous physical blow that she mustn't go on, using Gil Mayo as a substitute. Who wasn't anybody's substitute.

Shared interests, humour, wonderful sex . . . what more did she want? A home, yes. Children—well, maybe, she was still young enough, just—and he was more than willing to give her both. So why couldn't she take a deep breath and plunge?

She was miserably aware that she was demanding something, some perfect combination of attributes that simply didn't exist: Liam, romantic but unstable, shying away from decisions of responsibility; on the other hand Mayo, solid and dependable as the Rock of Gibraltar . . . and ultimately old-fashioned in his views on marriage. She didn't want to be—she *wouldn't* be—taken over, as part of his life, not wholly her own. Because there was ambition, too, soaring ambition of a kind she couldn't deny and he might not be able to go along with. She didn't see herself as a substitute, either.

Basically cool and sensible, she was detached enough to realise that this search for unattainable perfection might be an excuse to avoid commitment, to avoid the conflict between marriage and private expectations. But when all was said and done, there was the real, true reason, or rather, two of them: there was Liam still between them—and though Gil hardly realised this himself, Lynne, who wasn't yet forgotten, exorcised. Alex wondered if she ever would be. Her dark, sleek head drooped. She wasn't making sense and didn't know how to.

He said, "I won't accept this. What's wrong with me?" The exact words she had used of herself, with a different meaning. Dear God, she couldn't bear it, seeing him humble. Correction, not humble at all, but sore and furious. An entirely understandable reaction. At that moment, if he had added only a small endearment, she might even then have succumbed and said it: "All right, Gil, why not?" But that wasn't his style.

14

The decor at Charlie Girl, the new unisex hairdressing salon on Peter Street, was painted in hi-tech scarlet, black and grey. The assistants were called stylists, and male and female alike wore freaked-out hairdos in amazing colours, and a weird assortment of baggy white cotton garments that gave them the appearance of refugees from some Indian ashram. Detective Constable Keith Farrar, who was newly married, only just out of their generation but worlds apart, could hardly tell one from t'other at first, nor even second, glance. The ear-rings and make-up meant nothing.

There wasn't much going on this Monday morning, he noticed. The framed certificates on the walls, announcing the abilities and prowess of the stylists—Nikki, Vikki, Tamara, Jacqui, Jon, and Craig—looked down on empty chairs. A tall thin person with feverish red eye-shadow and hennaed hair cut like a scrubbing brush swanned towards him, a label pinned to a non-existent bosom, declaring herself to be Sam. It was only the absence of an Adam's apple that decided Farrar on the gender.

"Mrs. Who?"

Sam's disinterest was total. He'd known it was going to be hard going before he began, by the bored, dismissive glance at his regulation haircut and "straight" clothes, by the hostility aroused when he presented his ID, not by any means the usual reception accorded to Farrar, who was blond, smooth, and good-looking. And he knew it.

He repeated the name, and after some insistence, she was persuaded to look back through the appointments book to December 22. "Oh, yeah, she was here. She was Nikki's lady." A prominent notice declared Nikki to be the leading stylist and colourist. She cost three pounds more.

"Could I see her, please?"

"Nikki!"

She was older, wildly orange-haired, and a little more forthcoming, but not much. She didn't *exactly* recall a Mrs. Saville. Well, a lot of people had been coming here just the once, to try the salon out, like, and just before Christmas they'd been specially busy. He couldn't expect her to remember everybody.

He described the dead woman and showed her photo.

"We-ell, maybe her face is familiar, sort of. What d'you want to know for?"

"She's been murdered, love."

"You're joking!"

"Afraid not. Haven't you been watching the telly?"

"The stuff they were showing over Christmas? No way! We stocked up with videos. I never watch the news anyway; it's dead boring."

Well, at least it wasn't seeing the face on the screen that had run bells. "Come on, see if you can't jog your memory somehow."

Nikki's voice was plaintive. "I wish I could, but I really can't— I'm sorry."

"Thanks, love, that's a great help," Farrar said gloomily.

"No need to be like that; I've done my best. Anyway, I must've done her if she's in the book, mustn't I? There's no cancellation. And like I said, I do faintly remember her, but not exactly."

A concentrated frown appeared between the plucked arched brows as she pored over the appointments book. She'd never remember. Anyone over twenty-five very likely looked the same to her, Farrar thought, but she said suddenly, "Hang about, it's coming back to me, I had Mrs. Philips in at half past, one of my regulars, and I remember her saying what lovely blond hair that last lady of yours had, and asking if I couldn't do hers the same. Well, I told her it was natural, and *she's* been every colour under the sun, Mrs. Philips; shouldn't think she remembers what her natural colour is—"

"Good girl—you remembered! And you'll be able to tell me what time Mrs. Saville would have left?"

"Just before half past, it would've been."

Farrar smiled and closed his notebook. "Well done, darling."

"Be my guest." Nikki fluttered her eyelashes. Maybe he didn't qualify to join the wrinklies yet. Sort of sexy, really, these older men.

"Tell you what," she remarked as his hand was pushing open the plate glass door, "you could do with a cut and blow-dry yourself while you're here—why don't you?"

It was at times like these that Farrar understood the bloke who'd declared himself too old to dance and too young to die.

Mayo had walked into the station that morning to find trouble coming at him from all directions, as if Lavenstock's criminal element was suddenly making up for lost time, choosing, right on target, the beginning of what looked like being a flu epidemic here at the station, with men and women on the strength going down like flies.

Alex was taking a few days off as part of her entitlement, which precluded the prospect of an immediate meeting. Not that they had parted on bad terms. He though sourly that he might have felt better if they had. No, they were two mature adults, weren't they, and had ended up rationalising the bloody position so that neither was satisfied. In effect, they were back to square one, with nothing resolved, a situation he'd noticed often happened when you argued with women. But not for long, he told himself. He wasn't a man to live with unresolved situations.

He hadn't been too surprised when Alex had made what for her was evidently a momentous revelation. The possibility that she'd flown to Lavenstock from involvement with some man was one which had occurred to him more than once. What had surprised—and angered—him was her refusal to accept his insistence, his *promise*, that marriage needn't limit her freedom. A career if she wanted it—or a family. But she was like a lot more women in these enlightened days, he reflected bitterly; she wanted to have her cake and eat it. Whereas he only wanted her as a wife, not as a mistress. He was old-fashioned enough to find neither the sentiment nor the phrasing of that amusing.

A murder enquiry naturally took precedence over anything else, but juggling with several other investigations at the same time was a necessity you had to learn to accept. With regards to the Saville case, there wasn't much he need personally occupy himself with at the moment. The results of the forensic tests hadn't yet come in. Nor had the answer to the telephone enquiry he'd made in New York, the outcome of which couldn't reasonably be expected until tomorrow. Routine matters he could leave to others, while he got stuck into the most pressing of the new cases, amongst which were an overnight break-in at one of the leading jeweller's shops in the town, and a report of cocaine being passed at a teenage party. He plunged into the crisis, and succeeded in taking his mind off his personal problems for a few hours.

But lunch-time arrived with an incipient headache which he hoped to God wasn't heralding flu for him as well, and no ease to his soul. He took two aspirin and found himself snapping at Kite for no good reason, demanding to know what the hell Farrar was doing. Why wasn't he back from that hairdresser yet? It was only round the corner, wasn't it, not the bloody north pole? He heard the injured note in Kite's voice as he answered that Farrar was just typing his report out now, and checked himself sharply. No way to carry on. Whatever private miseries he'd had, he'd never before taken them out on his subordinates. "Bring him up, Martin," he said, feeling shabby. "I'll have it from him in words I can understand, not his A-level English."

"Mind how you go," Kite warned Farrar. "His Nibs has been like a bear with a sore backside this morning."

But the detective constable's succinct report, confirming that Fleur Saville had indeed kept her hair appointment in Peter Street, earned him an approving word, and Farrar, who was out for promotion, notched himself up another score.

When he and Kite had gone, Mayo walked to the window, brooding. His office overlooked Milford Road, busy as usual with the one-way traffic speeding through. Another day of raw damp, and though the snow had all but gone in the town centre, pedestrians were still muffled against the cold. Within his vision was the pet shop on the corner of Peter Street where it curved back on itself to run parallel with the main road, also Woolworth's and the

flower-seller who sat under the arched portico of the Victorian
Gothic Town Hall, surrounded by a burst of colourful pot plants
and baskets of daffodils and tulips from the Scillies. Fleur Saville
had loved flowers, had filled her house with them . . . He
frowned, dismissing the non-sequitur, trying to connect. Something wasn't right.

She had been alive at two-thirty and had, therefore, died some
time during the next half hour—presumably at home. Had she
really intended leaving Saville? The removal of her jewellery indicated she had, but if so, the absence of a note worried Mayo. He
thought Fleur, a woman to whom words and extravagant gestures
were everyday currency, would have left one. Unless she'd been
prevented by her murderer, there perhaps by pre-arrangement?
During that half-hour the phone had been answered by a man—
not Saville, since he was undoubtedly in his shop. And what about
the car seen outside? Was it one owned by the murderer—or was it
conceivable that he'd had the nerve to use Saville's car to transport
his wife to where she'd been found? But remember, she hadn't
been dumped until after six o'clock, so if the car had been bor-
rowed from the garage without Saville's knowledge, how had it
been returned? He'd been home before five. Or had it been used
merely to get the body away, transferring it to some other car
which had later been used to dispose of it? And did this indicate
collusion?

Mayo rubbed a hand across his face and, turning back to his
desk, caught a glimpse from the corner of his eye of a flying figure,
a mane of red hair. For an instant he thought the woman coming
from the flower-seller with her arms wrapped around a large azalea
in a pot was Zoe Henderson, but no. When she turned, he saw a
young girl he didn't recognise, no more than seventeen. He stared
after her as she disappeared with springy step around the corner.

He must make time somehow to have another word with Mrs.
Henderson.

The inquest on Fleur Saville was held on the following day and
adjourned for further police enquiries. By that time, the door-to-
door enquiries had been completed. They were predictably un-

helpful. No-one, it seemed, had noticed anything out of the ordinary on the day in question; and it was certainly too long ago for anyone to remember whether they'd happened to see Saville's own car standing outside his own house. Confronted with questions about his car, Saville had steadfastly refuted all knowledge of its being taken out of the garage that day.

After the inquest was over, Mayo decided to pick up the clock he'd spoken to Zoe Henderson about. If he was going to see her, he would get her to look at the damaged case with a view to having it repaired, which would be an incentive for him to get it working again. He drove home straight from the court.

The owners of the large house in which Mayo's flat was situated were an elderly couple called Vickers, a brother and sister whose family home the entire house had once been. David Vickers, retired from his business as tax inspector, his children dispersed to various parts of the globe, had lived alone in the house, uneasily and in some disarray, for a considerable time after the death of his wife, until his sister Freda, headmistress of the local girls' school, had also retired and consented to come back to share their childhood home. Of an eminently pragmatic and energetic turn of mind, unlike her brother, she had made conditions before moving in, and then immediately set in motion what she had been trying to persuade him was the sensible thing to do for years. Within a very short time the large house had been split up into three self-contained flats, quiet and respectable tenants found, and their own furniture ruthlessly thinned out to make the ground-floor rooms into a comfortable and easily run establishment for two people getting on in years.

Their original tenants had changed once or twice over the next ten years. At present the first floor was occupied by a married couple called Brownlow, with Mayo occupying the top floor, having successfully passed Miss Vickers's stringent tests as to what constituted a good tenant. The arrangement suited them all very well. The elderly brother and sister derived a certain amount of assurance from having a policeman in the house, and Miss Vickers enjoyed entertaining Mayo to the occasional meal. She was sure he must miss his daughter, as she did herself. She'd taken pleasure in their little chats, which she said helped to keep her in touch with the younger generation. Mayo in turn liked the couple's unintrusive friendliness, the fact that his sitting room overlooked a pleasant garden which he had no need to tend, and the freedom of having his own private entrance.

He was just putting his key in the door of his own apartment when Freda Vickers, hearing him, came out with a parcel she'd taken in with her own mail. From the handwriting, and the parcel's battered state, he deduced it was the Christmas present from his sister he'd never received, and from the powerful perfume issuing from it, that it was a broken bottle of the kind of after-shave he couldn't be sorry had broken.

Miss Vickers was deploring the carelessness that had caused this. "Posted well before the last Christmas posting date, too."

They exchanged opinions on the general fallibility of the post office system, and then she said, "I heard about the murder this weekend, Mr. Mayo. Has the culprit been found yet?"

Mayo replied that he hadn't, surprised at her question. She had always shown tact about his work, not expecting him to talk about it, and was certainly not the sort to be avid for lurid detail. Her next words, however, quietly said, explained her interest. "She was one of my girls at Princess Mary's, you know. I taught her for several years."

"Did you now?" He looked at Freda Vickers, neat in her check tweed skirt and dark blue cardigan jacket, wearing an impeccable cream silk shirt and gold chain, her becomingly styled grey hair, her soft, elderly skin enhanced by discreet make-up, encountered a shrewd look from her bright blue eyes, and made a decision.

"May I talk to you about her?"

She wasn't a woman for prevarication, and he had a feeling she'd anticipated, even led the way to his question. "Certainly. Can you spare the time now? My brother's gone down to the bank, and I've just made a pot of coffee."

He followed her into her tranquil room overlooking the back garden, carpeted in gold Wilton, with long powder-blue velvet curtains at the windows, and some excellent gold-framed water-colours on the walls. Little, shining polished tables stood about, covered with knick-knacks, except for one which held a coffee tray laid with silver, delicate china, and two chocolate digestive biscuits. She fetched another matching cup, saucer, and plate, and another two biscuits. The coffee was pale and lady-like, but the biscuits were good, dark, plain chocolate.

"What can I tell you about Fleur, Mr. Mayo?"

They'd known each other for nearly six months, were good neighbours and friends, but he was still Mr. Mayo to her and always would be. It was inconceivable that she should be anything but Miss Vickers to almost anyone.

"Things in general—what she was like, anything you can remember." He was confident she'd know the sort of thing. She was still remembered and respected in the town as being an excellent headmistress of one of the best and most renowned schools in the county, and from personal acquaintance he knew her to be a woman with an open and active mind.

"Where shall I begin?" She nibbled her biscuit, then put it down as if she'd suddenly lost the taste for it, sighing. "Well, frankly, I have to say that Fleur was a big disappointment. She came to the school on a scholarship, but then never quite came up to the promise she'd shown. When I first heard of her success as a writer, I was pleased for her and gratified that her years at Princess Mary's hadn't after all been wasted, though I must confess myself astonished. Until on reflection, I realised there was nothing surprising about it, that telling stories was the one thing she was uniquely fitted for."

Taking up her rose-patterned cup, she sipped gently and watched him over its rim.

"You mean she was a liar, Miss Vickers?"

"That's a little too strong. It implies deceit—and no, she was never really deceitful, I'll give her that."

But you didn't like her, thought Mayo.

"Let me explain. Her parents, Mr. and Mrs. Adams, were a very ordinary working class couple. Deeply religious people, and very strict, as I recall. Good parents in their own lights, but undemonstrative and rather joyless, and totally lacking in imagination. They could never have understood that a girl like Fleur, an only child, might be very lonely and desperate to have attention and affection lavished on her. The result was that Fleur, when she first came to the school, used to—what's the current jargon for it, fantasise?—about herself to the other girls, make up stories about exciting places she'd been to, well-known people she'd met, even claim that she was really the daughter of someone famous. It's a situation not as uncommon as you might think; many imaginative children do romance from time to time, and coming from such a drab environment . . . her name was really Frances, you know; Fleur was what she called herself, but I didn't insist."

"The other girls must have known she wasn't telling the truth? Didn't it make her unpopular?"

"Of course they knew. Even eleven-year-old girls are not fools; nor are their teachers. I made it my business to know everything that went on between my girls, Mr. Mayo." It amused him the way she spoke of "her girls," in the manner of Miss Jean Brodie. "But if they took her up on anything, Fleur would just laugh and say, 'You didn't believe all that, did you? Surely you knew I'd made it all up, just for fun.' And I suppose it was fun in a way, and harmless, if you knew you mustn't ever take anything she said seriously. At any rate, she never seemed to lack friends."

"I've met one or two of them."

"Let's see if you can recognise any of them from this." She rose and crossed the room with neat, decisive steps, returning with a leather-bound album from a drawer. It stayed unopened on her knee, however, when she sat down again and said in a low voice, "She wasn't perfect . . . but whatever could she have done that caused her to die as she did, Mr. Mayo?" and then, almost immediately, "I'm sorry—that's a very improper question which I hope you won't answer."

"I won't, because I can't. I only wish I did know."

She stared at him thoughtfully. "It was thought to be rather smart to be in Fleur Adams's set, you know. As she grew older, there was a circle of girls who always seemed to gather round her —not only girls who were easily led, either. I suppose she had what's called charisma; I used to think they found her style rather glamorous and wanted to copy her sophistication."

She found a place in the album on her knee, then handed it to Mayo. A dozen or so seventeen- and eighteen-year-old girls were seated around a Miss Vickers who was perhaps at that time a possible fifty, though not looking noticeably different from the present Miss Vickers.

"My sixth form, with my head girl sitting next to me."

"Gillian Challis, of course," Mayo said, instantly recognising the tilt of the head, the confident smile, and the hockey-playing physique of the future magistrate and governor of her old school.

"Gillian Lingard-Smith, as she was then. But no. No, it's the girl on my other side who was head girl."

Mayo transferred his gaze to the girl on the right of Miss Vickers. She must have moved when the camera shot was being taken, for the image was very slightly blurred, but he knew who it was. "Fleur?"

He looked up in surprise and met Miss Vickers's bright, speculative look.

"Yes, Fleur Adams. One of the very few judgemental mistakes I made in my career—at least, one hopes there were few. At the time, I felt that her qualities of leadership might be put to better use, that learning to use them for the good of the school might make her a little less—shall we say, self-centred? I'm very much afraid it didn't."

"Later, though? Of recent years, she'd put a lot into working for good causes."

"So I'm told, so I'm told." Her tone was dry; her blue eyes told him she had her reservations. He was reminded of Zoe Henderson's assertion that all Fleur's apparent benevolence was a boost to her own ego.

"Perhaps I didn't consider it carefully enough. At the time, as well as other considerations, it seemed to take me off the horns of a dilemma, from having to choose between Gillian and Nell Radlett."

Mayo searched the photograph again, and it didn't take him long to pick out a smiling girl with dark curls. "Nell Fennimore?"

"Yes. One of the cleverest girls of her year, Nell, with a place waiting for her at Oxford, and how does she end up? Wasted, married at eighteen, a mother within a couple of years. If Nell hadn't got herself tied up with Gerald Fennimore, what might she not have become? Ah, well. I daresay you're thinking I'm banging my drum, and you'd be right. There's nothing wrong with a home and children if that's what you want. I used to tell my girls; but for goodness' sake get yourself qualified first. But Nell—though she was a level-headed, sensible, and responsible sort of girl—never had quite enough ambition."

"Why not Gillian?" She had 'head prefect' written all over her. "What was wrong with her?

"Oh, nothing wrong, goodness no—except that she was *expecting* the honour to fall on her. That's not always very good for the Gillians of this world; things come too easily for them. You understand me?"

"Yes, I think so. I think you must have steered the situation through very tactfully. At any rate, the three of them seem to have remained very good friends."

"That doesn't surprise me. Gillian was brought up to put a good face on things. People's good opinion was always important to her. She took the disappointment well, got her head down and concentrated on her A-levels. Not much sense of humour, Gillian, but uncomplicated. Clever and competent. She got a good degree. And Nell had a very sweet nature."

Mayo drained his insipid coffee and stood up. His thanks to Miss Vickers were sincere, though she herself seemed to feel she hadn't been much help.

"I've said a lot about Fleur's drawbacks, haven't I? Perhaps not enough about her good points—and she had many. I must confess I was hurt at the time by her failure to respond to the faith I put in her—but I came to realise afterwards it was just as much a failure on my part to understand. I could never really *like* her, you see, however I tried, and when one comes down to it, everything she did was due to a need to be loved. Poor Fleur. I wonder if anyone ever understood this?"

15

The telephone was ringing as he reached his flat. Kite was on the other end. "Glad I've caught you. We've somebody here at the station you might want to listen to before you see Mrs. Henderson. I think we may have a lead."

Kite went on to tell him what it was all about, and Mayo said, "Hold it, I'll be right there."

The landlord of the Jolly Farmer at Corston Green came into his office wearing a cravat tucked into his open shirt neck, well-polished conker-brown brogues, and a navy-blue blazer with brass buttons. He was of middle height, with a luxuriant moustache, receding hairline, handsome in a 1940s RAF way, a man by the name of John Drury, who had come forward to report having seen Fleur Saville and a man together.

"At least I think it was her. Don't get much time for watching television, but there's always a bit of a lull in trade after Christmas, so we had it switched on in the bar last night, and I saw the photograph you've issued. I'm pretty certain she was the same woman who was in my place one night before Christmas with a man. She was wearing a red coat then, as well."

"Before Christmas? How much before?"

"As a matter of fact, it was the fourteenth of December, the Friday. The reason I can pinpoint it is we had a private party in for a meal that night—get a lot of them around Christmas. About a dozen women who work together in the same office had booked, and when she came in, at first I thought she was one of them. I directed her into the corner where they were having a drink before their meal, but she got a bit uptight and said no, she certainly wasn't with them, she was waiting for a friend. Well, I could see she wasn't their sort when I looked—she had real class, and very noisy they were, but you can't throw business away these days, can you?"

Mayo agreed that you couldn't. "Can you describe the man?"

"Hard to say. We were pretty busy at the time, and anyway he had his back to me most of the time. Big chap, though, I can say that—your type, come to think, yes, very much like you, black hair and heavily built. You to a T. Not somebody you'd like to meet in a dark alley on a dark night." Drury sniggered a little.

"Hmm." Mayo's face showed he didn't share the joke.

"Anything else you remember about him?" Kite asked. "Specs, for instance? Heavy, dark-rimmed ones?" Mayo threw his sergeant a sharp look.

"He wasn't wearing glasses at all that I remember."

"What time was it, and how long did they stay?"

"Oh, not long. Only had the one drink. Maybe about half an hour; round about the eight o'clock mark's the nearest I can say to when they came in. She'd be about five minutes earlier than him. One other thing that might help, though—my barman was out at the back when this chappie drew up into the car-park. I didn't see him arrive, myself, but Len swears he was driving a Jag. Pale grey or silver. They didn't leave together. I don't know how she came, but she telephoned for a taxi to take her home."

"Challis," said Kite, when Drury had gone.

"Drury said the man wasn't wearing glasses." But Challis, of course. Mayo's objections were token.

"We don't know that Challis wears them all the time."

"And he was in Zurich on the twenty-second."

"We don't know that for certain, either. We've only his word for it. And he drives a silver XJ6."

He did, he did. Mayo had detested Challis from the moment he set eyes on him, but up to now, he'd scarcely been in the picture. There'd been nothing to connect him with the dead woman. He'd said he hardly knew her. Mayo considered that gratuitous piece of information, annoyed with himself on two counts. Firstly, that he hadn't picked up the bloody silly remark on Sunday, recognising it as a lie; and secondly, that he'd misinterpreted Gillian Challis's reaction to it. At the time, he'd thought the agonised glance she'd cast her husband had been a plea for him to stay and give her moral support, whereas she must have been wondering what the hell had made him come out with such an obvious lie. Of course Challis must have known Fleur, and pretty well, if she'd been such a close friend of his wife's all those years.

The idea that had been forming in his mind began to take substance, and as other facts began to click into place, his thoughts went racing ahead. He knew that the case had shifted into the right gear at last. He was as sure in his own mind as he could be that Challis was the man seen in the Jolly Farmer. And therefore the man who'd been at Kelsey Road on the twenty-second? Steady, not so fast, he told himself, but he was tense with excitement. It began to look as though this was the break they'd been looking for.

"I want to talk to him," he told Kite, "and have that taxi driver traced who picked Mrs. Saville up—if it was her." Then, as Kite had his hand on the doorknob, "Do I really look like that arrogant bastard?"

"We-ell." Kite stood in the doorway considering his glowering superior. "Not really. It's the sweetness of the expression that makes the difference."

Later, Mayo asked for a call to Browne Moulton, the City firm of merchant bankers where he assumed Challis to be this Tuesday morning, and was channelled through a series of secretaries with upmarket voices before being told Mr. Challis was in conference, but would ring him back if it was important.

"It's important," Mayo said. It was a couple of hours later that Challis came on the line.

"What can I do for you, Inspector?"

"Chief Inspector," corrected Mayo, who scarcely ever bothered about rank, cutting short the apology with a brief request for an interview with Challis. "As soon as you can make it," he said. "Perhaps this evening, at your house?"

Challis put in quickly. "Oh, no need to go to that trouble. I'll call in and see you on my way home, if that suits you?"

Mayo smiled, grimly satisfied. He'd got precisely the reaction he'd anticipated. He'd have been much less happy if Challis had agreed to see him in the presence of his wife. He arranged to see him about five-thirty, which meant Challis, he calculated, having to start out from the City at not less than half past three. Either Challis's working day wasn't as long as Mayo's, or he was suddenly anxious to appear co-operative.

"Please sit down, sir." Kite indicated a chair in front of the desk behind which the chief inspector sat.

"Thank you. Mind if I smoke?

Mayo, a reformed smoker himself, did, but had resigned himself to the fact that it was necessary to allow others to smoke at times. He didn't keep an ashtray in the room, however, a small disapproval which was made manifest by his pointedly asking Kite to produce one. It took Kite some minutes, and Challis looked of two minds, by the time this performance was over, whether to light up or not, as was intended, but his need evidently triumphed. He made a flamboyant performance of it, with a cigarette drawn from a gold, monogrammed case—Mayo couldn't remember when he had last seen anyone using such a thing—and a lighter to match. He was wearing with his formal business suit a very dark blue shirt with white stripes and a white collar and cuffs, accentuating his dark, two-shaves-a-day complexion.

"Well," he began eventually, with a self-conscious half-laugh, "I know why you want to see me—can't pretend otherwise."

This man made too many bloody assumptions, Mayo was thinking, when Challis astonished him by adding, "It wasn't very wise of me to lie to you, but I didn't really see that it mattered one way or the other that I wasn't actually in Switzerland on that Saturday —well, not the whole day, that is."

"I see." Mayo's face was expressionless. From the corner of his eye, he saw Kite's Biro arrested in mid-air.

"The thing is—well, I flew back to London early on Saturday morning. My wife was meeting me with the car at Elmdon Airport, so later in the day I took a train up from London to the Birmingham International Station, then got myself across to the airport to coincide with the arrival of the seven o'clock flight from Zurich."

"Very neat," commented Mayo. And crazy to have admitted such a thing before he was asked. Never explain, never apologise—hadn't he ever heard the dictum? Shrewd, but not clever, Challis, and soft at the centre. Too anxious to save his own skin to be thinking clearly about the situation. "And what had you been doing with the rest of the day?"

Challis dragged at his cigarette. "This is all very embarrassing. Do I have to say?"

"Yes."

"Well then, if you must. The truth is, I spent the day in London."

"So you said. Doing what?"

Challis looked rueful. "With my secretary, as a matter of fact . . . you know how it is. I'm sure she, er, won't have any objections—not in the circumstances, you know—to confirming it."

I'll bet she won't. I'll bet she's the sort of secretary who'll agree to anything, probably thinks it rather a lark to get one over on the fuzz, thought Mayo, who remembered the Roedean voice and recognised a lie even when it wasn't jumping up and hitting him in the face.

"You can check, if you like."

"Oh, we shall, sir, we shall. What's her name, where does she live?"

"Her name's Carrington, Jane Carrington; she lives in Notting Hill, I think, but that doesn't matter—we weren't at her place. I have a small penthouse flat over the offices which I use if I have to stay in London overnight."

Did he, oh, did he? Mayo wanted the address all the same, but Challis apparently couldn't remember it. He promised it the following day, after which he said, "Right, then," stubbing out his half-smoked cigarette and if Mayo wasn't mistaken, looking mighty relieved.

His hands were on the chair arms to lever himself up ready to go when Mayo said smoothly, "I'd like you to clarify one or two other points for me, if you would, Mr. Challis, while you're here."

Challis looked suddenly wary, raised his eyebrows. "Such as?"

"Such as where you were on the fourteenth of December—in the evening, that is."

The only indication of surprise was the slightest flicker of a nerve at the corner of his mouth. "The fourteenth of December?" Challis puffed out his lips. "That wouldn't present too many difficulties, if I had my last year's diary with me."

"Try to remember, sir. It was a Friday."

"Oh then, I can tell you. I was almost certainly playing squash, at the club round the corner from my offices. I stay on late to play most Friday nights, unless I have another engagement."

"What time did you get there?"

"It's usually around seven. I have a game and then a shower, possibly a drink afterwards. Yes, I'm almost certain I played that night."

"Who with? Who was your partner?"

"Ah, there you have me. I'll need my diary for that."

"Did you win?" asked Kite.

"I don't remember that, either, but I usually do." Challis smiled, completely at ease. "Now, if you don't mind—" His hands, with the black onyx ring on his wedding finger, were again on the arms of his chair. "I don't know what all this has been about, but I hope I've been able to satisfy you."

"Not altogether. Because you were seen, at around the time you claim you were playing squash in London, in the Jolly Farmer at Corston Green, with a lady we believe to be Mrs. Fleur Saville."

Mayo was taking a chance, speaking as if this were, in fact, established, though the taxi driver hadn't yet been traced, but Challis, after a longish silence during which he first adjusted his glasses, then his tie, didn't even attempt to deny it.

"All right," he admitted at last, smiling ruefully. "It's a fair cop. I was with her, yes. We just went out together a few times, had a bit of fun; nobody was hurt. You know how it is," he added, using what seemed to be a favourite expression of his, but no, Mayo didn't know how it was. He wasn't one of those who winked at this sort of shabbiness.

"Quite the ladies' man, Mr. Challis. First your secretary and now Mrs. Saville." He ignored the man-to-man smile. "Well, here's another question I'd like you to answer."

"Another?" Challis shot his wrist, revealing an inch of pristinely laundered cuff. His watch, too, was heavy, chunky gold. "Oh, dear. Well, fire away."

"What can you tell me about Candace Neale?"

This time the silence lasted perhaps fifteen seconds. A space of time, out of all proportion to its quality, that was compounded of electric tension, fear, a suspension of being, as if a clock, or a heart, or the world had stopped.

Then Challis ran a hand through his hair, reached for his cigarettes again, withdrew his hand. "Candace, did you say?" His voice was without a tremor. "Candy Neale? That's a name from a long way back. From Oxford, as a matter of fact. I met her when I was up there. She's an American."

"Is? You've renewed your acquaintance recently?"

"Not to say renewed it, no. But as a matter of fact she's in publishing now, back in the States, an editor in the house that published Fleur. They met not too long ago, and when she knew where Fleur lived, she asked her if she knew me—and sent her regards."

"How good a friend was she?"

"Very good. But not in the way you mean." Mayo said nothing, merely looked and waited. "Christ, she was just one of the set I went around with; there was nothing more to it than that!"

Mayo smiled. At last he'd got Challis rattled. "Let's just go over your movements on the weekend of the twenty-second again. Correct me if I'm wrong on any point. You came home from Zurich early Saturday morning, right? Stayed in London until late Saturday afternoon, then took a train from Euston to the Birmingham International Station, arriving at what time?"

"Six-fifteen. It was late."

"Then you went to the airport. How'd you get there?"

"By that new Maglev—that new hover thing."

"Where you were met by your wife—why not your chauffeur?"

"Because he's only expected to drive me during the week—look, what the hell is all this? If you're trying to lay this murder on me, you're bloody—" Challis

"Well, Mr. Saville?"

"Oh, go to hell!"

Mayo said blandly, "We shall need to see you again, sir, I'm sure, and there'll be certain formalities, such as signing your statement and letting us have your fingerprints before you go, but that'll do for now. They'll be destroyed afterwards," he added, "if necessary," and had the dubious satisfaction of seeing Challis open his mouth as if to protest, and then thinking better of it.

Kite returned from escorting Challis out and walked over to the window, where he stood staring at his own reflection in the darkened glass, superimposed upon the spectacle of the neo-Gothic Town Hall and its turreted clock tower, its floodlighting each night giving it a romantic appeal, like soft evening lights on an aging woman's face, quickly dispersed by the light of day.

"What's on your mind, Martin?" Kite turned round.

"I'm not sure. Except that it seems all wrong to me. Mainly because Challis doesn't strike me as being one for the women. Rugby, squash—that macho type's more at home with his own sex. And I don't mean . . ."

"I know. And if it's any consolation, I've the same doubts about him myself. Sutcliffe said she wasn't one for the men, either—but that apart, I'm sure there wasn't anything of that sort between the two of them. He was far and away too glib about it—and I'm just as sure he was lying when he implied he was having it off with his secretary as well. I've no doubt she'll give him an alibi, though— jobs with Browne Moulton are probably worth a fib or two."

"And for another thing, what's with all this confession about not being in Zurich? Jumped the gun a bit there, didn't he? Which you don't do unless you've plenty to hide."

"He's impulsive, friend Challis. Speaks without thinking, maybe acts that way, too."

"You mean he panicked? Yes, I suppose he guessed he'd been seen with Fleur in the Jolly Farmer, and that's why we wanted to see him. And of course he'd know we'd be able to check his arrival from Zurich easily enough, so he thought he'd better establish an alibi first off, for the twenty-second. Because he was actually up here, in Lavenstock, committing murder?"

"So you do see him as a murderer?"

Kite dug his hands in his pockets. "Given the right circumstances . . ."

Emptying the ashtray onto scrap paper, Mayo screwed it up and threw it in the waste basket and went to open the window. A blast of icy cold air lifted the papers on the desk, but no way would he chance getting cancer from inhaling Challis's second-hand cigarette smoke. After a minute, he closed the window and went back to sit at his desk.

"Who's Candace Neale, by the way? You scored a bull's eye there."

"Just an idea I had, may come to nothing, but Challis's reaction was interesting. Bear with me, Martin, I've put some enquiries out in New York, and when I get an answer I may be able to put you in the picture." As if on cue, the telephone rang. Mayo looked at his watch. "Maybe this is it—I'm expecting it about now." He stretched out a hand, and after a moment, he nodded at Kite in affirmation.

Kite went out, and when he eventually returned, he was triumphantly waving a sheaf of papers, but he was given no chance to speak. Mayo was leaning forward tensely over his desk. "Martin, we may have him, motive and all."

"Motive?"

"Fleur Saville had something on Challis. I think she was blackmailing him—though nothing so crude as money for her own needs. Remember those thumping great donations the Challises made to the Buttercup Club fund? Okay, other people have been generous, too, but not to that extent. I'm willing to bet Challis was paying that money to buy her silence."

"About what? Had they been having an affair, after all?"

"It goes much farther back than that. I'd rather not say anymore because until I've seen Candace Neale, it's still largely speculation," Mayo admitted. "Apparently she's in London at the moment, and I'm hoping to fix up an interview with her tomorrow."

Kite said, "I've got these reports—"

"Just a minute, Martin, hear me out. You come in later if I'm wrong—but how's this for a scenario?" Mayo tipped his swivel chair back, sank his chin on his chest, and squinted down at the toes of his brown leather lace-ups, polished like conkers. He wasn't fussy about his clothes, but he was about his shoes. A psychiatrist might have made something out of that. "Supposing Challis set up the situation, coming home a day early from Zurich, providing a fictitious alibi with his secretary, and making elaborate arrangements so his wife wouldn't know, then his being the murderer is a distinct possibility—and, logistically speaking, no real problem. If this was what happened, the murder must have been premeditated —but how did he hope to get the opportunity? Presumably he knew Fleur would be fully occupied all day, since his wife's day was similarly planned. But what if they'd *agreed* to meet, for the same reason they'd met at other times? Maybe she stipulated Kelsey Road, and at that particular time, because she knew Edwin would be at the shop, Gillian out of the way at the church hall. It wouldn't have mattered after all if she'd been late back after the lunch break; she could always have found some excuse for it. And he agreed to meeting her there because it was the best time to murder her? All he had to do was to hire a car at the airport to get there and back—if it happened to be one of similar colour and shape to Saville's, that would be enough to account for Mrs. Tennyson mistaking it for his—she's not expert."

"I think," Kite said, "you'd better see what I've got here, before you go on."

"What is it?"

"The lab reports on the prints found on the desk at Kelsey Road, also the report on Saville's car. The car's clean . . . in a manner of speaking. That's to say, it probably hasn't been cleaned for weeks, but there's no trace of his wife having been transported in the boot, no blood, fibres, nothing. They found one or two of her hairs and some fibres, not from the clothing she was wearing that day, on the upholstery of the front seat, but they would, wouldn't they, if she was used to being a passenger? There were her prints, of course, and his, all over the place—and more besides, the same ones that were on the desk."

"Identified?"

"Michael Saville's. The missing son."

Not Challis. *Michael Saville.*

The results of the enquiries Kite had put out about him had come in together. "After he left home, he seems to have followed the fag end of the hippie trail for a while, in various parts of the world, and maybe that was what made him think this country wasn't so bad, after all. At any rate he came back and bummed around for a while doing whatever job he could find. Ended up working as a baggage handler at Heathrow, only he handled the baggage a bit too personally, see? He was sent down for twelve months."

That was why his name was in a police dossier; that was how his fingerprints had been traced. It also accounted for Mrs. Tennyson's mistaking his voice on the telephone for that of Edwin Saville: fathers and sons often have similar voices. That was what Saville had been hiding, Mayo was sure. He must have suspected that Michael had been at the house that day and kept quiet about it, even to the extent of falling under suspicion himself.

So how did all this fit in with the case he was all set to make out against Challis? Depending, of course, on what he might learn tomorrow. For to London he would still find it necessary to go; he felt it in his bones. But his certainties had been shaken. He just hoped he hadn't been guilty of jumping to conclusions, making the theory fit the facts, something he was forever warning Kite against. He didn't like Challis—it was a personal antipathy from which he couldn't escape—but God forbid he should let that cloud his judgement.

On the other hand, he hoped his judgement hadn't been faulty.

"Where's Michael Saville now?"

"Apparently he's going straight, has a job with a software firm in Leamington."

"Got his address?"

Kite nodded, and Mayo reached for his jacket. "Let's go; we might just catch him in, then."

16

Leamington Spa. A Regency town, pleasant, bland, with wide streets and public gardens, white classical facades, at its best in the sun. At seven o'clock on a dark January evening, however, with the broad, well-lit main shopping parade left behind, the quiet terraces and crescents had a cold and deserted air about them, though the houses themselves, enviable, owner-occupied, and well-groomed, offered glimpses of tastefully lamplit interiors, or spoke of quiet comfort behind their drawn curtains. Along the road into which Kite turned the car, on the other hand, the street lamps served only to emphasise the peeling stucco and general shabbiness of its large flat-fronted houses, mostly converted into flats inhabited by the very young or the very old, the disadvantaged or members of ethnic minorities.

The young woman who answered their ring at the door of a top-floor flat in a run-down terrace house midway along one of these streets spoke abruptly, in an uncompromising manner that went with the straight brows and the dark hair cropped close to her head, with the way the door was opened but left on the chain. "He's not in," she told them.

"Then perhaps we could wait."

"He might be some time."

"We're in no particular hurry," Mayo answered pleasantly. "And anyway, we'd like to talk to you as well." She gave him a quick, vivid look through the aperture. Mayo didn't think she was surprised to see them, but she made them wait, accepting their IDs with the chain still on the door and then ringing the Lavenstock police station to confirm they were who they said they were.

"You can't be too careful," she said as she finally admitted them to the flat. Mayo agreed that she had done the right and proper thing, though privately he didn't think it was caution that had led her to act as she had done, rather a desire to set the tone of the interview, to show them she knew the score.

A savoury smell of something cooking issued from behind a door in the corner; the table was laid with a lace cloth, cutlery, and glasses for two. The young woman herself wore no make-up, a black jersey, and a dark, flowered woollen skirt. He judged her age at about twenty-eight and her attitude towards the police as touchy.

In the event, they had no sooner entered than footsteps were heard running up the stairs, a key was inserted in the lock, and a young man of about the girl's own age came in, a bottle of wine in his hand. Scarcely pausing when he saw the two policemen, he put the bottle on the table, crossed the room, and drew the girl towards him with an arm around her shoulders.

"Mr. Michael Saville?" Mayo asked. The other acknowledged the question with a barely civil nod.

"It's the police, Mick," the young woman said.

"I'd noticed. What do you want?" He had his father's tall, lanky frame, light brown hair that fell forward over his brow, a handsome, sulky face, and an insolent manner. "I hope you haven't been giving my wife any hassle."

Kite stiffened, but had the sense to keep quiet.

Mayo hadn't previously noticed the wedding ring on the young woman's small brown hand, but when he looked now he saw that it was new. He said stolidly, "Are you aware, sir, that your step-mother, Mrs. Fleur Saville, has been found dead in so far unexplained circumstances?"

"That's the good news. So what's the bad?"

"That why you're celebrating?" Kite asked, waving his hand towards the wine bottle on the table.

Saville laughed. "Celebrating? No—but we might well be. I hated her guts."

"Mick!"

"It's true, Jane; you know it, and I don't suppose it comes as any surprise to these—gentlemen—here."

"Cut it out, Saville," Mayo said quietly. "We've a murder on our hands, and we're not here to waste time, ours or yours. Just you answer my questions. Shall we sit down?"

Saville shrugged, threw himself on to the sofa, tugging his wife's hand to sit beside him, and left the two officers to find seats for themselves. "For starters," Mayo said, settling himself composedly, "we know that you left home several years ago after a quarrel with your stepmother. And you've never been back since?"

"Damn right I haven't."

"Except, of course, on Saturday, December 22 last, the day Mrs. Saville was murdered? What were you doing there?"

"Interesting question," Saville drawled, cool as you like. "But if you think, in view of my past record, which is no doubt why you're here, that I was there with felonious or murderous intent, you're mistaken. I was there legally, availing myself of what was mine by rights."

"Explain that, please."

"Mick means," began his wife. "No, Mick, let me tell it." There was a plea in her voice that Mayo guessed was far from habitual with her, and perhaps that was why Michael Saville shrugged and let her go on. "It was because I persuaded him to go and see his father. It *was* Christmas after all, and I thought it was an appropriate time to tell his father we were married, and to arrange for us to meet."

"For Jane and my father to meet, not *her*," Saville said. "All right, I'll take it from there, Jane." His arrogance seemed suddenly to drop from him, and with it something of his good looks, revealing a weak mouth and a slackness of feature that would become more evident with the years. The strong one in this couple was the girl; he was lucky, thought Mayo, to have found her. "I've never had any real quarrel with my father, and although we were never all that close, we've kept in touch, on and off, since I left home. I wanted him to get to know Jane, to know that since I met her, things are beginning to go right for me, at last. We've both got good jobs—Jane's teaching A-level science, and I'm not doing badly in computers. Anyway, I drove over, the Saturday before Christmas, and went to see him at the shop."

"What time?" Kite asked.

Saville smiled faintly. "I know he never changes his habits, so I timed it to arrive at one, when he'd be shutting the shop up. I was glad I'd gone; he was like a dog with two tails when he saw me, but all the same he looked ghastly—in a terrible state, he was."

"Sick, you mean?"

"That's what I thought at first, but it came out gradually that it was because of her. She'd come up with some crazy idea that morning about him selling his business and going to live abroad, and they'd had a row about it. Can you imagine it, my father retiring, giving up, leaving the only things that have ever mattered to him? It would've killed him inside a month—though come to think of it, maybe that would have suited her. But he was worried sick, and I could see why. If she wanted something, she got it in the end, no sweat." He stopped and said, "Look, I'm having a drink. Want one?"

"No, thank you."

Jane Saville walked across to a cupboard, poured a small tot of whisky, and brought it back to her husband. "Go on, please," Mayo said. "What happened then?"

"Nothing. We just sat in the back and drank some coffee. It was a long time since we'd seen each other and we'd a lot to talk about. We sat there discussing various things until it was time for him to re-open."

"Neither of you went out?"

"No. He didn't even answer the door. Somebody knocked about ten minutes before he was due to open, but he ignored it."

"And at half past two?"

"He opened the shop, and I went to Kelsey Road to pick up several things. That's what we'd been talking about, in and amongst. When she started throwing out all my mother's belongings, Dad had salvaged one or two small bits and pieces"—he gestured vaguely round the room—"things she didn't think worth selling even, and put them up in the loft in case I ever wanted them. I said I'd take them back with me that day. I left it till half past two because I'd no desire to bump into her, and he'd told me she'd be at the church hall by then, playing at being Lady Bountiful, organising some sort of charity do for kids."

Bitter lines pulled down the corners of his mouth into an ugly expression whenever he spoke of his stepmother. Mayo noticed that never once had he referred to Fleur as anything but 'her.'

"So you drove down to Kelsey Road at two-thirty—"

"No, I walked. I drive a Cavalier, and I couldn't have got all the stuff in that. We arranged that I'd leave the Cavalier in the public car-park in the centre, so that if my father wanted it he could use it; I'd use the Granada to take the furniture home and bring it back the next day, leaving it in the yard behind the shop. Which is what I did, dropping the house keys back at the shop on my way home."

"What time would that be?"

"Half past three, something like that? I don't really know."

"And your father was there, in the shop?"

"Sure."

"Why did you answer the telephone when you were at Kelsey Road?"

"The telephone?" He hadn't expected that one, a flash of surprise, even fear in his eyes. "Oh, yeah, I remember," he said too late. "Reflex action, I guess. I was thinking about—about something else entirely, but it didn't matter, did it? I was there quite legally."

"In Mrs. Saville's study? What were you doing in there? It contained nothing you were 'entitled' to, legally or otherwise, did it?"

"No?" The immature petulance of Saville's face had set into savage lines. "Only the one thing I wanted most, the French secretaire —the one possession of my mother's that even she couldn't bring herself to get rid of. But there was no way I could have taken it with me; it wouldn't have gone in the Granada with all the other things, for a start."

"And?"

"That's all. I locked up, left the keys with Dad, and drove home."

"Are you sure that's all? Your stepmother died approximately between two-thirty and three. When you were in the house, are you sure she didn't come in unexpectedly, that you didn't meet and quarrel, that you didn't kill her?"

"Of course I'm bloody sure!" Saville wheeled round to his wife.

"You see—what did I tell you? If you don't believe me," he shouted to Mayo, "you ask that woman across the road—that Mrs. Henderson. She was in the house when I got there, gave me the fright of my life. She'll tell you."

Zoe Henderson! "What was she doing there?"

"She said her telephone was out of order, she'd come across to use theirs."

"She had a key?"

"She didn't fly through the window." He saw Mayo's face and added sulkily, "She told me she keeps a spare, because my father's wife had been known to lock herself out on occasions."

"Which rooms did you go into?"

"All of them, if you must know. I used to live there—remember? It used to be my home, my mother's, I wanted to see it again . . . but I took nothing, nothing except these things from the loft." He sprang up and went round the room, touching each article as he went. "This, and this, and this!"

Mayo took no notice of the histrionics. "When you were in the main bedroom, did you notice any jewellery on the dressing table?"

"Yes, I bloody did. And fifteen pounds on the kitchen table. And I didn't sodding well take either!"

"Watch your language, Saville," Kite warned.

"I didn't ask you if you took it," Mayo said. "I asked if you'd seen it."

"I've said I did."

"Describe it, please."

Saville looked sullen. "A couple of rings, I think, and something else—oh, a necklace or a bracelet of some sort, some kind of red stones."

"Neither your father nor Mrs. Henderson have mentioned anything about you being there, Mr. Saville. How d'you account for that?"

"Because *they're* part of the human race," burst out Jane Saville. "They probably anticipated how you'd react, and they were right, weren't they?"

The silence in the car lasted until they were through Warwick. "I wouldn't put it past him," Kite said eventually. "That he did it, I mean, and his father and Mrs. Henderson were shielding him."

"I think his father may believe he did. That would account for his lies about his car. But my money's still on Challis." The excitement had returned. Mayo was feeling much more confident than he had before he saw Michael Saville. The visit had cleared away some of the debris that had been hampering their progress. He couldn't see yet exactly how things were likely to go, but one thing he was certain of—Challis's past was about to catch up with him. After that, they'd have to take it from there.

"I'll tell you what else I think, Martin. I think the excuse about Mrs. Henderson's telephone being out of order is a lot of poppycock. She was in that house for another reason. Not necessarily to murder Fleur Saville—she'd have had to be pretty nippy to have done so and got her out of sight, maybe into that van of hers, within the time limits—but I reckon she'd seen something which had aroused her curiosity. Whichever, we're about to find out."

They were doomed to disappointment. When they got back into Lavenstock, both Mrs. Henderson's house and the other one down Kelsey Road were locked up and in darkness.

17

American executives in large publishing houses came less thrusting, perhaps younger at first glance than Mayo had expected, until he remembered that he was privy to knowing how old she actually was. Slender and elegant, an ash-blonde with brown eyes, Candace Neale had a sideways smile that was charming and a firm handshake. Her voice, when she spoke, had warm overtones, yet he sensed tension in her. "What can I do for you, Chief Inspector Mayo, Sergeant Kite?"

She'd taken the trouble to get the names and ranks exactly right. Mayo was impressed. "Good of you to see us, Miss Neale. I realise you haven't much time, so I'll get straight to the point."

"Oh, I've fifty minutes before take-off, and I'll be happy to fill in the time. I do a lot of flying, but I'm still not overjoyed about it. Sitting around thinking about it beforehand makes it worse. And of course, in a situation of this sort—"

They had met with official permission in one of the empty departure lounges at Heathrow, with time to go before her flight left for New York. Outside, aircraft took off and landed, one a minute. Rain belted down onto the tarmac from a uniformly leaden sky. Foreign tourists walked by to other departure gates, not looking sorry to be leaving behind what England had recently been throwing at them in the way of weather.

"Thank you, I appreciate your co-operation. Shall we sit down?"

When they were seated, it was she who began the conversation, albeit hesitantly, by asking just what she could do to help. "Because you do realise I hardly knew Miss Lamont—Mrs. Saville, that is? I only met her once."

"And that was here in London on the third of July last year, I understand?"

She nodded, passing her tongue round her lips. "That's right, I believe that was the date."

"It's that meeting I wanted to ask you about, first of all." Mayo was watching her carefully. "Something you discussed there interested her very much, and I'd like you to try and remember if you can what you talked about."

He wondered if the palpable nervousnesss she was showing was really due to her phobia about flying or to something else. Her fingers kept on twisting the narrow strap of her black leather shoulder-bag into a slip-knot, then pulling it out. "I'll help in any way I can, but you must realise I can't break a confidence."

"There can't be any question of keeping confidences when it comes to murder. And Mrs. Saville is dead."

The slip-knot came free again as the strap was pulled tight. "I wasn't actually meaning her . . ." She stopped and plunged into her bag for cigarettes.

"Let me make it easier for you. On Saturday, the twenty-second of December, you met Bryan Challis, here in London."

He'd counted on the bluff, the educated guess—call it what you will—coming off, and it did. "Did he tell you that?" The cigarette lighter was stayed in mid-air.

"We've spoken to him, and we know you met," he answered ambiguously.

"I see." She paused, smiling faintly, and some of the tension went from her face. "It seems to be my fate to meet people at airports. Yes, sure, there was a couple of hours between his flight arriving from Zurich and mine leaving for New York, so it seemed logical to meet here, have a drink together, and talk about old times. Salad days and all that."

"Old times in Oxford, when you were students together?"

"What else?"

"About Fleur Saville, perhaps. And the fact that she was, to put it bluntly, blackmailing him?"

For a moment he thought she was going to refuse to answer, or at any rate evade his question, but she said cautiously, after giving him a swift, uncertain look, "That was what he implied, yes."

"How long have you know Bryan Challis?"

"I hadn't seen him for nearly twenty-five years. I knew him at Oxford; we went around in the same set for the two years I was there, but we've never met since—not until he contacted me."

He had to ask her a question that might be an impertinence, but he thought she would answer it truthfully. She had clear eyes that reminded him of Alex's. Candace. The name suited her. "Were you lovers, Miss Neale?"

She regarded him gravely. "We had—a relationship, yes."

"And as a result of that, you had a child."

"You *have* been doing your homework!"

"We have a copy of Mrs. Saville's letter to you, after you'd met. She mentioned your proposed visit to Lavenstock. I made enquiries and found you'd left Oxford sooner than you'd intended, that a daughter was born to you shortly afterwards."

From below, a Concorde lifted off into the air, a big predatory-beaked bird with backswept wings. "I don't really see what relevance all this has . . ."

"Miss Neale, it isn't likely we should have troubled you, caught you in mid-flight as it were, if it wasn't important."

She lit the cigarette she'd forgotten until now, drawing on it with small, impatient puffs. "Okay, I'm sorry. Yes, I do have a daughter. But Bryan Challis isn't her father. Anything between us was over long before I got pregnant, from the moment he met his wife, in fact."

He couldn't believe it. He strove to keep the shock and chagrin from showing on his face. He'd been wrong—and what was infinitely worse, so sure he'd been right. If this woman was telling the truth—and he'd swear she was—and Bryan Challis wasn't the father of her child, then his motive for murdering Fleur Saville had vanished. Everything had seemed to fit—the dates, the coincidence of the two women meeting, the unlikely sums of money paid into the Buttercup Club fund. Mayo had never for a moment doubted that Bryan Challis would have done more than murder to prevent this sticky little bit of his past coming to his wife's ears. With any other wife, he might have ridden out the storm, but with Gillian . . . Mayo thought that in Bryan Challis's shoes he too might have trembled.

"Are you sure?" he asked, trying to swallow his disappointment. "Sure?"

"I'm sorry." He rubbed a hand across his face. "I'm not in any way doubting your word. You've surprised me, that's all. Please go on."

"My child's father was a fellow American. But you know, the idea of being a father appalled him, and he'd absolutely no intentions of marrying me—which was the luckiest break I ever did have, though I sure didn't think so at the time." For the first time, he noticed grey in the ash-blond of her hair, faint lines at the corner of her eyes that weren't all laughter lines. It was absurd, the comparison, but into his mind floated the image of Lola Tennyson, shoulder to shoulder with this woman from another kind of life, another continent. Life was rotten sometimes, but it would never beat either—they'd always fight back. Like Lola Tennyson, Candace Neale too had courage. Her mouth lifted again in her attractive, crooked smile as she leaned forward to stub out her unsmoked cigarette and continue her story. "I went home, and it was tough for a while, but I don't regret it. My daughter Karen's the best thing that ever happened to me."

Mayo thought about his Julie. He smiled at her. "That's nice." He went back to what she'd said, about the end of her affair with Challis. "So you know Challis's wife as well?"

"Knew. We were very good friends. Oh, I'll admit it, I was so jealous when they first met—he obviously had no eyes for anybody else, and who could blame him, she was so stunning? But I got over it, one way and another. And later, when the baby was on the way, that's when I really got to know her . . ."

Gillian Challis was still a very good-looking woman, with her dusky-peach complexion, her blond hair. And clever too. She must have been, to get to Oxford and take the good degree Miss Vickers had spoken about.

"She was pretty wonderful to me at that time," Candace Neale was saying. "I guess I wouldn't have gone through with it, having the baby and all, if she hadn't persuaded me how wrong it would be to have an abortion. She was a lovely person, but very intense, with strong moral principles—and of course that's why they mar-

ried. Sex without marriage would have been out of the question, at
least as far as she was concerned . . . it actually bothered her that
most people thought they were 'living in sin,' as she put it. God,
nobody would have cared either way! We all slept around in those
days, didn't we? In a way that really shocks my daughter's generation."

Mayo inclined his head in a non-committal way. Not all, he
thought. Some had a bit of self-control, a touch of the Puritans if
you like, or maybe they were just more particular. Especially people like Gillian Challis. He said, "Then why didn't they say they
were married? Why the secrecy?"

"Oh, he couldn't let it be known, in case it got back to his father."

"He needed his father's permission to marry?"

"Well, not that, but his approval I guess, and in the circumstances, he didn't want to hurt him."

"What circumstances?"

"His father was dying, Mr. Mayo. There'd apparently been
somebody else lined up for Bryan to marry, before he went to
Oxford, somebody with a bit of money, and a good Catholic. The
way Bryan put it to me was that he couldn't do that to his father on
his deathbed—tell him he'd married someone else, I mean. Bad
news whichever way, especially with her not being a Catholic and
all—"

"Not a Catholic?" intervened Kite. "But—"

"Oh." She looked unhappily at the two men. "Oh, I guess you
didn't know about Ruth either."

Mayo felt as though his brains had been scrambled. Ruth? he
thought. *Ruth?*

A jumbo jet roared off the tarmac. Candace Neale watched their
expressions while the sound died. "I'm sure you understand about
these old Catholic families better than I do. Or maybe you think
it's impossible, people still having these sort of attitudes, this day
and age?"

Mayo did not. Looking at the world around him, he couldn't
believe bigotry and religious prejudice had died with Oliver Crom-
well. But that wasn't what was concerning him at the moment.

"Let's get this straight. Challis has been married twice? Then his first wife died?"

"Not that I know of."

"Divorced, then?"

She gave him a level look. "They must have been, mustn't they?"

With his Catholic principles? Unlikely—unless they weren't so strong that expediency hadn't got the better of them.

"At any rate, he and Ruth pretty soon split. I don't know exactly why—she was very upset and wouldn't talk about it—but anybody could see even by then that their marriage was a fairly total disaster. They'd basically nothing in common, and with hindsight I can see it just couldn't have lasted. He went overboard for her, I guess because of her looks, and he's hard to resist when there's something he really wants. She looked real sexy, you know, but she was about as . . . well, anyway, there are some women who should never marry at all, and I think Ruth Whittaker was one of them. She told me once she couldn't understand all the fuss people made about sex, and if she'd listened to herself, she wouldn't have married. Does this make sense?"

He nodded. It was becoming clearer every minute. "What happened to her, then? What happened to Ruth Whittaker?"

"I don't know; we lost touch. When I asked Bryan the other day, he said she'd gone out to the Far East to work with homeless children, and that figured; it was fairly typical of the sort of thing she'd do. I'd written her several times, to let her know about the baby and so forth, but I never did have an answer."

"Let's go back to my original question—how much of all this did you tell Fleur Saville when you first met her?"

"When I found out she came from Lavenstock, I mentioned I had friends who came from there, and it turned out she knew Bryan Challis well. I was really pleased because with this merger in my company, it was on the cards I'd be over here a lot and I thought it would be kind of fun to look them up again. I even mentioned that I'd probably bring Karen over with me and we'd visit. I asked about Ruth. She looked amazed. 'Ruth?' I remember exactly the way she said it. 'But Bryan's wife is called Gillian,' she said. By this time I realised I'd put my foot right in it—I figured there must have been a divorce, but maybe he'd kept it quiet, perhaps even from this Gillian. Later, I recalled that was the name of the girl he'd been going to marry. I was surprised about the divorce, though, because at the time I knew her, Ruth didn't approve of it either. She was very strait-laced, and well, you don't have to be a Catholic, or even very religious, I guess, to believe marriage is forever. But people change: they meet someone else, they lose their faith . . . for all sorts of reason they might have agreed to it later. Anyhow, I began to backtrack fast, but I guess she realised there was something fishy, and she must have ferreted it out. After all, she was a journalist at one time, wasn't she?"

"Yes," Mayo said. His thoughts had taken on an entirely new turn. He had his motive now. A different one and possibly more powerful.

Gillian Challis might have been able to swallow, with a struggle, the fact of an illegitimate child of her husband—but a previous marriage was a different kettle of fish. She would never knowingly have married Bryan otherwise. To a woman such as she was, with a strong Catholic conscience, marriage would be indissoluble except by death. On the other hand, his first marriage was unlikely, in the circumstances, to have been blessed by a Catholic ceremony and therefore wouldn't have been recognised as a marriage at all by her church, so the question of whether he was divorced or not would have been largely irrelevant. As far as the church was concerned, that was. As for the law, Bryan Challis might be in very hot water indeed.

"So when you met Challis, what did he say about his divorce?" Kite pressed, taking up Mayo's thoughts with the kind of telepathy that their working well together was sometimes apt to induce.

She avoided looking at either of them. "That's something we never got around to discussing, I guess. All he wanted to talk about was exactly what I'd told Fleur."

Mayo didn't doubt her word that it hadn't been mentioned, but if not, he didn't think it likely to have been an oversight. Candace Neale was no fool; it was very probably something she'd rather not know—and something Challis certainly wouldn't have volunteered.

"I'm sorry, that's my flight call," she said as a voice came over the loudspeaker. She was beginning to gather her things together, but slowly, as though there were still things she wanted to say. They stood and shook hands; Mayo thanked her again.

"I don't know about that, Mr. Mayo. Right now, I feel a heel. Maybe I'll see it differently when I've had time to think it over— but look, there's something I have to know. You're working on Bryan having killed Fleur, aren't you?"

"It's a possibility we can't rule out," Mayo replied cautiously.

"Oh God. If I hadn't spoken to her about him, she'd still be alive."

"No. If she hadn't *used* it, she might be. There's a difference."

He hoped he'd succeeded in convincing her.

18

The rain streamed down the windows in torrents, hammering on the roof-tiles of the old stable that was now the garage. It was so dark she'd had to switch the lights on already. She pressed her hand to her aching head and wished Rollo would stop that eternal barking. He hated to be shut up in the garage, but she wouldn't have him in the house when she was preparing meals, when his nose was level with the kitchen counter and everything in the way of food was grist to his mill.

Despite her aching head, she moved efficiently about her well-equipped kitchen, preparing for the dinner party that evening. She'd never felt less like entertaining, but Gillian's feelings always came second to her sense of duty, and the Hammonds had been booked for tonight for weeks. Even if Fleur was dead, appearances had to be kept up; life had to go on.

So, like that other well-conducted person, she went on cutting not bread and butter but cucumber, slicing it rapidly, in the correct, professional manner, the razor-sharp Sabatier knife following her doubled-up fingers with speed and assurance. She arranged salad attractively round the cold salmon trout on the large, flat silver dish, decorated it was aspic jelly, and expertly piped mayonnaise. She always took the trouble to learn how to do things the correct way; it was so much easier in the end, she told Penny. And Bryan liked things to be done, and people to behave, properly. He wouldn't like the Hammonds to think his wife was going to pieces just because her best friend had died. He would have preferred to keep from them altogether that she had died in such sordid circumstances.

The salmon trout went into the fridge, covered with clingfilm; she turned round and without warning, there in the middle of the kitchen, the tears began to pour down her cheeks. There was no way she could stop; the enormous painful growth that had been swelling up inside her for weeks had finally burst. She sat down at the table, her head in her hands, and with dry racking sobs, let her grief have its way, but when the tears eventually stopped, she felt no better. She got up and poured cooking brandy into a tumbler, hiccuping as half of it went down in one gulp.

She'd known there was something wrong with her marriage from the first. If she was being honest—and now, if ever, was the time for honesty—she'd known even before she walked to the altar with him. But his charm—such a false charm it had turned out to be—had blinded her. She'd even become a Roman Catholic for him when they got engaged—and, like most converts, had become more devout than the devout, embracing a faith that had in the end been the truest and most abiding source of comfort in her life.

But she should never have done it, never have held Bryan to the promises made before he'd gone to Oxford, and she to Durham. They'd met at her cousin Elizabeth's twenty-first birthday party, and it had been love at first sight, or at least that was what she'd thought. But by the end of the first year it was evident, to her at least, that their engagement had gone sour on him. He *could* have backed out, of course; there was essentially nothing to stop him, except that it would have needed some courage, and Bryan always took the easy way out. And also, his father had died by then, leaving unexpected debts and the business in a bad way. Bryan had needed her money, the money her parents had settled on her. Not a large sum, but enough to cancel the debts and put him back on his feet. She'd had no illusions, she'd known this, and had traded it for marriage, shutting her eyes to the consequences. She'd believed that because she loved him that didn't matter, and had had to live with the fact that it did for a long time. Because once done, it was too late. Marriage in the sight of God was once and forever.

She drained the rest of her brandy, stood up, and, leaning against the sink, stared out of her kitchen window, across the saturated lawn, towards the great stand of yews that she'd always hated, they and their implacable circle of darkness. Why hadn't she asked Bryan to have them cut down? He would have ordered it to be done straightaway, if she'd ever told him how much she disliked them. She only had to beckon, lately, and he'd do as she asked. It was one of the things which had first made her suspicious. He wasn't naturally a conciliatory person. Another thing was the ostentatious presents he gave her and Penny. That and the over-generous donations to the Buttercup Club, when money, as she knew, was tight.

Why, she had wondered, had he suddenly found such sympathy with a cause he'd hitherto shown minimal interest in? One *she* hadn't been able to interest him in, but Fleur had, she now realised. Did he think she was such a fool that she'd accept this apparent change of heart without wondering why?

There were so many trees here at the back of the house. Beech and the yews and some tall elms that had escaped the Dutch elm disease. Dejected rooks cawed and sat in melancholy huddles, high on their bare, dripping branches. The rooks avoided the yews, as did the plants, which refused to grow in their shade; Gillian, like the plants, hated darkness.

She was afraid of the dark. Not afraid of the night, which until recently she had welcomed as a friend who brought sleep and forgetfulness—but afraid of the darkness of beyond, of eternity, of damnation, to which the sins of omission and commission would condemn her. She had known; she had condoned Bryan's sin for too long. She had been jealous of Fleur all her life, lovely traitorous Fleur, who struck the match that had lit the furnace. Though she had truly loved her, too.

How long had she been existing in this limbo? Looking for reality, when there was none, no sense in trying to find it. It had been a long and lonely road. She found her hand clenched round the cook's knife, her knuckles white. Slowly she made herself unlock her fingers, and the knife dropped with a clatter to the tiled surface. It was denied her, the oblivion she longed for; the great quietus, it was denied her. But she had thought she had reached the limits of her endurance before, and she had gone on.

When Kite rang Challis at his office from Heathrow, he was told Challis was seeing a client in Birmingham and wouldn't be in the office until the following day. The trip into the City was therefore unnecessary, thank God. Mayo didn't fancy a noisy and tedious journey, jostling and jockeying for position with bad-tempered drivers and wet, scurrying, risk-taking pedestrians in London's overcrowded city streets. Instead, after leaving Heathrow, the car's nose was headed for home.

Kite drove. It gave Mayo an opportunity for silent thought, since Kite, who was a good driver, swift, decisive, and alert, with his mind on what he was doing while he was on the motorway, didn't talk too much. Mayo was glad of it; he was in that keyed-up state of mind when he knew he was at the end of a case, when the quarry was in sight. His adrenalin was running high. He had the motive, and the murderer, though the proof was something else. He thought he might even have the means, and the why and how of the jewellery left on the dressing table. There were still aspects that were puzzling him, though . . .

The going had been slow out of Heathrow and up the motorway, with the heavy rain and several contraflow systems slowing up traffic, but now they were into the cross-country Warwickshire roads and lanes. The steady downpour had spread north, washing away the last traces of snow. The sodden earth could take no more, and water lay in miniature lakes at the sides of the road. There were sounds like tearing silk as the tyres hit water, and the headlights in an afternoon as dark as night picked out the dark-humped shapes of hedges rushing urgently past. Fauré, passionately pure, poured into the interior of the car from Radio Three.

"Very enlightening, all that, wasn't it?" Kite asked presently.

"Puts a different complexion on things, certainly."

"Only I don't see how . . . ?"

"I don't myself yet, not entirely. But pin your ears back and listen, and then let's see what we come up with," Mayo answered, reaching for the radio OFF button.

For the rest of the journey home, they took the case apart, and by the time they got there, they'd reached what seemed to be an inescapable conclusion.

Gillian heard the Jaguar crunch down the drive and swing round towards the front door, where it set Bryan down, before continuing towards the garage. Rollo was going frantic. A moment later, freed by Turner, he was hurling himself back and forth between the front door and the kitchen door as he always did, past the study window where she sat, tearing himself apart with indecision and his impatience to get indoors at last. She heard Turner lock the garage, then crunch away towards his cottage, Bryan's footsteps in the hall and his shout to Rollo, the slam of the kitchen door. They came into the study together, man and dog, both large, blustering, and noisy. There was a remarkable similarity, too, in the pugnaciousness of the big Airedale's square jaw to that of Bryan's, rather more evident at this time of day, when he needed his second shave and a drink.

"What's that you're doing?" he asked, giving her a duty kiss and then immediately performing his routine of crossing to the drinks tray and pouring himself a substantial scotch.

"Nothing special. Bench work." She turned over the sheets of paper on which she'd been writing, knowing he wouldn't be interested enough to comment further.

"God, I'm tired," he said. "Good thing I'm home early; maybe I'll have time for a nap before the Hammonds come. It is tonight, isn't it?"

"They're not coming."

"Oh? Nothing wrong, is there? I thought Rodney looked a bit off-colour last Friday—"

"They're all right, as far as I know. I put them off."

She had imagined she had herself under control, that he wouldn't notice anything untoward, but the look he gave her quickly disabused her of this. "Put them off? Something *is* wrong. You don't look well yourself. Is that what it is?"

She'd managed to erase all signs of tears, but there was nothing she could do about the pallor that lay under her fading tan, giving her a sickly, sallow appearance. She'd rubbed off the blusher she'd never before needed on her cheeks after putting it on; however she applied it, it stood out, making her look like a clown.

"I didn't think you'd want them around with the police here," she answered his question. "And I hardly imagined they'd have been and gone before the Hammonds arrived."

"Police? Here? What are you talking about?"

"Oh, Bryan, what do you *think* I'm talking about? Fleur's murder, of course. What else?"

Silence hung between them. Then, incredibly—or perhaps not so incredibly, because Bryan always got what he regarded as his priorities right—his first question was "What did you tell the Hammonds?"

"You don't need to worry about that," she said dryly, in spite of her hurt. "I didn't tell them the *real* reason—and anyway, here *are* the police."

19

The rain had stopped. The winter pansies outside the front door at Boxwinder House had survived the frost and were lifting drenched heads in small, glowing pools of yellow and lavender and purple. After the temperatures to which they'd all lately grown accustomed, the early evening seemed to Mayo to hold an almost spring-like softness.

On this their second visit, they were shown into an oak-panelled, lamplit study, a small room with each panel carved in pointed arches to the ceiling, just off the vast hall. Like a lady chapel, thought Mayo, an impression strengthened by the monk's bench drawn up at right angles to the fire, and the silver vase of spring flowers set on a plain oak credence table. But the analogy fell short at the gas-coal fire flickering in the grate and the television set in the corner, the soft velvet furnishings.

Challis was drinking whisky, not his first if Mayo was any judge. He finished the glass off with a gulp and immediately poured another, effecting unconcern when Mayo declined the offer to speak to him in private.

"I'd like you both to be present, you and Mrs. Challis."

Mayo was watching, not Challis, but his wife, as he spoke, but there was no reaction from her, but for a small, stiff nod of acquiescence. She was sitting in a swivel chair turned round from a small desk in the corner. She looked ill. Perhaps she knew what was coming, too. He suddenly experienced a feeling of revulsion for the whole rotten business and the part he had to play in it, a momentary feeling, however, which he rigorously suppressed. He was doing what he was paid to do, what he believed in; if he entertained those kinds of doubts for long, he was in the wrong job. He was soberly aware that a family was about to be destroyed, but he

had an ultimately simple view of right and wrong: he didn't believe criminals should be allowed to get away with anything.

"There are questions which concern you both. If you don't
mind."

Challis shrugged. "As you wish."

Even with his capacity for self-delusion, he must have realised
what the presence of police officers here signalled, but he was going to bluff it out to the end, which Mayo could have predicted.
What he didn't try to predict was how soon Challis would collapse.
That he would collapse was certain. It was written in the character
of the man, in the way he'd let himself be carried along with the
flow of events, regardless of the rocks that lay submerged under
the water and might sink him at any time, until it was too late.

Mayo began as he and his sergeant lowered themselves into the
armchairs indicated. "I want you to go back to our last meeting,
Mr. Challis. We established then that you came from Zurich, not
on the Saturday evening of the twenty-second of December as
you'd led your wife to believe, but on the Saturday morning. Why
did you do this?"

"I've already told you why." He slid his wife a quick, cautious
glance. The look she gave him was blank and uncomprehending,
but he turned away, refusing to meet her eyes. No surprises here,
either, that he'd neither told his wife that he'd been questioned,
nor prepared her for what was to come.

"I-I'd arranged to spend the day otherwise."

"With your secretary's what in fact you said." Mayo had no
intention of letting him off the hook. "But we've reason to think
there was a different explanation for your returning early." Despite his effort at seeming indifferent, Mayo could see the man was
beginning to sweat. Moisture lay on his skin, which looked grey
and, with the dark shadow on his chin, gave him a villainous look.
"Truer to say, the reason was because that day you intended to
murder Fleur Saville, isn't it?"

"Murder her? No, it bloody wasn't!"

"Wasn't it? How was it then?"

"I told you why I came home."

"I don't believe you."

"That's your privilege. But how d'you think I managed to commit murder up here when I was in London?"

"Tell him, Sergeant Kite."

Kite cleared his throat. "Possibly because you weren't in London all the time. Let's say you'd previously arranged to meet Mrs. Saville at her home after lunch, just before she went back to the church hall. Say you hired a car in London and, having previously set up an alibi with your secretary, drove up here, murdered Fleur Saville, and dumped her in the lane near Seton End. Say you returned the car to the airport branch of the hire-car offices, waited until the Zurich flight came in, then simply walked out to where you'd arranged to be met by your wife, as if you'd just got off it."

"Say what you damn well like, that's a load of old rubbish, and you know it! What reason had I? Why should I want to murder Fleur Saville anyway?"

"Do you deny you were having an affair with her?"

"Yes—no, I—"

"Well, which is it? It was yes in your previous statement."

Quite suddenly, all the fight went out of Challis. He looked as though he were deflating slowly, like a limp balloon. "I wasn't having an affair with her. Christ, that's the last thing I would have done."

This time Mayo heard the catch of Gillian Challis's breath, almost a slight moan; her hand went to her throat. She averted her face sharply.

"Then why'd you meet her on December 14, to name but one time?"

Challis wouldn't answer. Mayo let the silence build up. The Airedale, sensing the tension of the humans in the room, got up and mooched restlessly round. It had mean eyes and a black-and-tan coat, curly as astrakhan. It walked across to Kite and began to nudge his notebook with its big, square nose. Gingerly, Kite moved the book away. The dog lifted its lips warningly. Its teeth were yellow; its breath was bad. Challis snapped his fingers, and it went reluctantly back to his side, where it sat with ears pricked, while Challis nervously scratched its boxy head.

"She wanted to persuade me into giving money to that club of

hers," he came out with at last. "She'd found out—something—
that happened years ago."

"Not to beat about the bush, she was blackmailing you."

"She didn't put it like that, not Fleur. She never threatened me
or *asked* for money; she just hinted. The first time all she said was
she'd met someone who was with me at Oxford. She understood,
only wanted to offer her sympathy, blah blah blah. She realised I
was young at the time, what it must have been like for me all these
years—God, as if anyone could know! It was Fleur at her most
sickening. Then she changed the subject to that bloody club of
hers, and how much it needed funds; she was sure I'd understand. I
understood, all right. I sent her a couple of substantial cheques.
But I might have known—she asked to meet me again, and this
time she was on about the new wing needed up at the hospital . . .
I could see it going on for the rest of my life."

"And that was when you decided to murder her." Like many
basically weak men, Challis would not act until cornered, when he
would be at his most dangerous, lashing out impulsively, without
thought or calculation.

"No! I didn't come home from Zurich to murder her; that's
crazy. I had to meet someone, on their way back to the States, and
the only way was to come back early from Zurich. I spent the rest
of the day at the penthouse flat—alone—until it was time to get the
train home. And that was *all* that happened."

"Except that the 'someone' you were meeting was Candace
Neale, wasn't it?"

After a brief struggle with himself, Challis admitted it. "Well, all
right, yes. What about it?" he added, managing to summon up a
touch of bravado, but he'd guessed what was coming. You could
smell fear on him.

"Why did you lie about this the first time we spoke?" Challis
shrugged.

"Hoped we wouldn't find out that Fleur Saville had threatened
to make your wife aware of the situation, didn't you? And had
therefore given you a strong motive for murdering her?"

"Gillian's name was never brought into it! I wanted to find out
just what Candace had told Fleur and how much Fleur was making

up. She told so many lies, you could never be sure with her. She'd said something the last time I saw her, about Candace's daughter, which made me think she might, possibly, be on the wrong tack— maybe she didn't know, after all."

"Didn't know what?" Mayo pressed.

Challis cast another agonised glance at his wife. "Can't we, for God's sake, go somewhere private?"

"Your wife's going to have to know sometime."

"I—I can't."

"This is one you can't dodge, Bryan," Gillian said suddenly. *"Who* is Candace Neale—and what was it I shouldn't find out?" Since that first involuntary movement, she had sat rigid and almost unmoving, looking like a marble statue, her face colourless, her patrician profile a classical cameo against the rich folds of the dark velvet curtains, with the light making an aureole around her blond head. Now there was a peculiarly charged concentration in the way she waited for him to answer.

He said nothing.

"It'll come better from you," Mayo advised, giving him the op- portunity to put it to his wife in the way he would know best, but Challis, who was beginning to look as though he was being ham- mered into the ground, only responded with a groan, sinking his head in his hands.

All right, he'd had his chance. "Mrs. Challis, your husband was allowing Fleur Saville to blackmail him because she had found out from Candace Neale, that twenty-five years ago, in Oxford, he married a young woman called Ruth Whittaker."

Seconds passed.

"Is that true?" Gillian's voice sounded peculiar, quite un- recognisable from her normally confident, magisterial tones. *"Is it true?"*

His bowed shoulders and the refusal to meet her eyes gave her the answer.

"Is she still alive?"

"I don't know—how should I? I've had no contact with her for years."

"How *could* you?" She was staring at him in a confusion of anger and grief and misery. And yet—surprise? Shock, yes, but disbelief? Mayo couldn't be sure. "How *could* you have married me when you already had a wife?"

"You mustn't take it so badly—it was all over, before you and I were married. It was crazy, a big mistake . . . but these things happen all the time. You know what people are like at that age; you don't know what hell I've gone through . . . I soon knew it wasn't going to work; that's why I left her—"

He was recovering, Mayo saw.

"Who was she?"

"Just someone I met—"

"And married."

"Not in church. She wasn't my wife, not in the true sense I mean, that is."

"You didn't even bother to get a divorce, I take it?"

"She wouldn't entertain the idea. Till death us do part, she said, and meant it. I think she'd some futile idea we might get together again."

"She wouldn't know you were keeping me as your second string, of course. That you'd let me go on waiting for you, all the time you were at Oxford. You've lived a lie and forced me to live one, too. Did you give no thought to what would happen to me if this got out?"

Self-absorbed, neither of them seemed to have given a thought as to what would happen to their daughter, either, Mayo thought grimly, and then was confounded when she added, "What about our child, what about Penny?"

Penny would be all right; she was young, with a strongly independent character, and a survivor, if Mayo was any judge from the brief but definite impression he'd gained of her.

"I—I'm sorry," Challis muttered, and the huge inadequacy of the apology seemed to sum up the failure of the whole of their lives together.

"Sorry—what does that matter? Shouldn't you have thought of that before?" Mrs. Challis had a bitter tongue and a look to match when the need arose. Yet her tone had changed; she sounded oddly apprehensive as she asked, "Are you going to charge him with murder, as well as—bigamy?"

Mayo stood up and walked past Challis to stand with his back to the fire, where he could better see the reactions of both of them. He said, "How much of all this did you know, Mrs. Challis? How much did Fleur Saville tell you?"

"Know?" In the face she raised to him he caught a glimpse of a secret, inner self, a naked look, gone in a second. She looked him straight in the eye. "Nothing," she said.

"Then what *was* the reason? Why did you kill her?"

The silence in the room hung thick as a blanket. Outside the rain overflowed from a blocked spout. The dog gave a low growl. Challis lifted his head, an expression of total disbelief on his face.

Gillian Challis swung round in the swivel chair towards the desk.

She was quick, buy Mayo was quicker. The knife glinted in the flames from the artificial coal, but almost on the instant she drew it from under the papers on the desk top, he was across the room, and had her wrist in his grip. A split second later the dog launched itself after him, and with an almighty crash they were all on the floor. The dog recovered first. Its jaws were within an inch of his throat when Kite got a stranglehold on its collar, twisting it from behind. At that moment, Challis came to life, taking charge of the animal and getting it out of the door.

When he came back, the two policemen were standing in the middle of the room, Gillian was sitting on the sofa, looking dazed, but without that frozen look she'd had ever since he came home. He sat down opposite her in silence, trying not to think about the moments before she'd made that lunge for the knife.

His glance ranged round the room, from the desk to the policemen, but the knife was nowhere to be seen. Had he imagined it? Gillian, with a *knife* for God's sake! Gillian, *killing Fleur?* He told himself, as he had done a thousand times, panicking now as he had done then, that she couldn't have known, how could she? And then remembered that she did now. Mayo had told her, and all pretence between them was over.

She began to speak, addressing herself to Mayo. "I was trying to write it all down for you—but I haven't got very far. There, on the desk. I knew you'd find out, sooner or later, and I wanted to get it clear, in case—in case—that day, you see, that awful day . . ." She closed her eyes, and it seemed as though she might not, after all, be able to summon up the strength to continue.

Kite shifted his weight. Mayo signalled caution. He recognised the guilty person's need to talk and knew its usefulness. The police station, the bare facts and stilted sentences of a written confession could come later. He sat down again, and Kite did likewise, opening his notebook.

"All right, Mrs. Challis. Let's have it. Everything. Take your time."

She opened her eyes. "Yes." Her voice was so low they could follow her only with difficulty. "We'd plenty of time, so we drove back to Lavenstock slowly, by way of Kennet Edge. When we got to the Edge, it hadn't yet started sleeting, and I—I didn't tell you the truth; we did get out for some air. There was nobody else about. She began to tell me about the quarrel with Edwin as we got back to the car, about some brilliant idea she'd had of selling up and going to live on one of the Greek islands, but that Edwin had dug his heels in and refused to discuss it sensibly. She said the row had gone off in other directions, and ended with him accusing her of having an affair with another man. She looked sideways at me when she said that, smiling in that way she had, as if she knew something you didn't. Well, it was true, she said, there *was* a man who was madly attracted to her. I said, 'Don't do this to me, Fleur,' and I told her I knew about her and Bryan, how I'd known it ever since he began to make those huge gifts to the Buttercup Club. I always read the accounts meticulously, and it came as a shock— he'd never shown any interest before, and why hadn't he discussed it with me, when he knew I was so closely involved? I realised it was conscience money, and I began to put two and two together."

She paused, clenching her handkerchief tightly in her fist.

"She wouldn't have it arranged any other way," Challis put in bitterly, "wanted it all above board, she said. Anyway, you were always at me to give more—at the time it seemed, well, at least you might think I'd at last done something that met with your approval."

Gillian glanced at him, then went on again as if he'd never spoken, as if he weren't there. The blood rushed to his face. "She just stood there by the car, putting a tragic expression on, and she said, 'Darling, I'm so sorry, you had to know sooner or later. But it's not how you think.' I could see—at least I thought I could see—that she was cooking up one of her wild stories and I—I just felt that everything was falling apart, my marriage, our friendship, and well, that was when . . . oh God, this time she was telling the *truth* and I didn't believe her! I didn't ever mean to kill her."

A rising note of desperation had crept into her voice towards the end of the flat recital of events. As if of its own accord, her glance travelled to the desk and fixed on what was there with something approaching panic. Mayo said, "Better if you let us take charge of that, I reckon."

He picked up her handbag carefully and passed it over to Kite. Square, chunky, with a heavy gold frame that formed a sharp right angle. She repeated, "It was an accident. I never meant to kill her." Her eyes, suddenly wide and horror-struck, beseeched him to believe her.

Perhaps not. Or perhaps not now, when remorse had had time to set in. Mayo watched her, half-convinced. But as he looked at the bag and imagined the fury that had swung it by its straps, given so much weight to the blow that the edge of the frame had bitten deep into the temple and killed Fleur Saville, he wasn't sure. At that moment—and for how long before that?—Gillian Challis had certainly wanted her friend dead.

"You were always jealous of her." Challis seemed to have forgotten they weren't alone—or else he was hitting back. She hadn't moved an inch towards him in understanding or forgiveness, and maybe he was beginning to be ready to wash his hands of her.

"Don't be ridiculous." But it was a truth that had evidently gone home, and this time she didn't make the mistake of ignoring him. "What reason had I to be jealous?"

"Because she always went one better than you, didn't she? She was famous; she'd more friends. You couldn't bear it that *you* weren't always top dog, that she got all the kudos. You've been jealous of her all your life. And then you thought she'd taken me."

Mayo, watching the hostility between them that was at last out in the open, thought this was probably the most acute observation Bryan Challis had ever made. Even Miss Vickers, wise in the ways of her girls, hadn't seen this. She had known that to Gillian Challis appearances were paramount, though. However unsuccessful her marriage had been, Gillian was committed to it through her religious beliefs, and she had made the best of it, in the same way as she had, years ago, made the best of her disappointment at not getting the coveted position of Head Girl. So Miss Vickers had said, who had thought her uncomplicated because she had been adept at putting on a good face or at hiding her feelings, depending on how you chose to look at it. Gillian Challis had her complications. If it was possible to love someone and hate them at the same time, he thought that she could. Hers had been a love-hate relationship with Fleur Saville. To the extent that when she killed her, she had possibly hardly realised why—or even whether it was Fleur or her husband she was subconsciously hitting out at when she swung that bag.

When, earlier that morning at the airport, Candace Neale had revealed to them Bryan Challis's long-guarded secret, two bare wire ends of thought had come together and flashed: how far would Bryan Challis go to prevent his wife learning of the one thing which without doubt would have destroyed his marriage?

Or, how far would *Gillian* have gone if she had known of it—if, for instance, that day, Fleur had told her the truth? To stop Fleur from using it, from making it public knowledge—as she, Gillian, must have know she was entirely capable of doing?

Suddenly that remark of hers had been understandable. "A soul in torment," she'd said. Applied to herself, Mayo guessed it wasn't far from the truth. Gillian, with her Catholic certainties, must have been shattered to learn of the continued deception which had struck at the very roots of her faith. And desolated by her uncharacteristic, uncontrollable response to it. A mortal sin, the penalty for which was spiritual death.

From there it had been a short step towards taking a succession of facts, unremarkable in themselves, but which, put together, had in the end assumed a significance that had made him certain it was Gillian Challis, and not her husband, who was the killer.

To what extent even now could they believe her story? She'd been suspicious for weeks that her husband had been having an affair with Fleur, so it wouldn't have come as any great shock to her to have it apparently confirmed. She claimed that she'd misunderstood Fleur over that, and maybe she had. She denied Fleur had told her of her husband's previous marriage, and maybe that was true. They would never know for certain, unless she chose to admit it, whether she had.

Nevertheless, driving back to Lavenstock by way of Kennet Edge—a bracing spot, certainly, but with nothing to recommend it on a morning as bitterly cold as that Saturday, other than the fact that it would have been deserted—indicated a degree of premeditation. Which one of them, in fact, had suggested getting out of the car, Fleur or Gillian? Certainly after Fleur was dead, she hadn't acted as an innocent woman, driven beyond reason to commit an act of folly, would have done. Wouldn't she have gone to the police, admitted what had happened? Gillian Challis wasn't a woman who would shrink from the consequences of a moment's loss of control. Instead, she had coolly bundled her friend into the boot of her car, and immediately gone about setting up an alibi for herself.

"How did she manage it?" Kite had asked. "If they left the White Boar at ten past one, Fleur must have died around half past, so how did she keep her hair appointment?"

"She didn't. It was Gillian Challis herself who kept the appointment, of course. And that was cool, if you like, but simple. Neither woman was known there; it was Fleur Saville's first appointment, so all Gillian Challis had to do was give the name of Saville when she walked in. She probably counted on the fact that if any checking-up was done, to most of these girls all middle-aged women look pretty much the same; it's the hair they look at, and there at least they were superficially alike, both with very fair hair, cut in a similar way."

"And that's pretty much what did happen, according to what the girl told Farrar," Kite said. "She was taking a risk, though. What if someone she knew had come in?"

"I don't think that would have deterred Mrs. Challis. It was an unlikely chance. I daresay she was probably prepared to explain that Fleur hadn't been able to keep the appointment and she'd taken it up instead. Then of course she would have had to rethink her alibi. But as it happened, she didn't need to."

He himself had noticed, when he saw them seated together in that school photograph, how similar they looked, two blond girls together. That had been just after he had stood at his window and watched the one-way traffic flowing past, and at the back of his mind had been Gillian's assertion that she had last seen Fleur's red coat disappearing into the hairdresser's—when it fact, driving along Milford Road from the right, sitting in her car, she couldn't possibly have seen the entrance to the shop, with Peter Street almost doubling back on itself from the corner.

"And when she left the hairdresser's, all she had to do was drive down to Kelsey Road, let herself in with Fleur's keys and leave the jewellery. It couldn't have taken her more than a minute or two to slip into the house, but that, if I'm not very much mistaken," Mayo said grimly, "was what Mrs. Henderson saw—Gillian's very distinctive white car. She was very likely on her way to the shop at the time and, being naturally inquisitive and taking an interest in Edwin Saville as she does, she used the excuse of her out-of-order telephone to go across and see what was happening. That would be when Michael Saville came in and found her."

"If she'd told us she'd seen the car there, she could have saved us a lot of trouble. Why the devil didn't she?"

"Who can tell what motivates a woman like Zoe Henderson? She detested Fleur Saville—probably thinks whoever killed her deserves to get away with it. She's devious, as well as a lot more things—Saville's welcome to her. Maybe she doesn't know about the penalties for hindering the police, but she's going to find out in the very near future—both she and Edwin Saville, though the reason he kept quiet is more understandable."

"It's like most problems, simple when you know the answer," Kite said. "If Fleur hadn't put her rings and her bracelet on the dressing-table herself, it must have been somebody else who knew of the quarrel. Somebody who saw the value of using them to indicate she had decided to leave Edwin because of it. The only other person who knew—apart from Mrs. Tennyson and, of course, Saville himself—was Gillian Challis. The thing that amazes me is that she was able to go back to the church hall, with the body in the boot, and carry on as though nothing had happened."

"Not only that—but drive home that evening with it still there, until she could dump it in the lane at Seton End on the way to pick Challis up at the airport. Maybe it was simply a convenient spot en route, but more likely she intended to leave her in the gravel pits and found the lane blocked. Remember telling me about a case last year, an uproar over a possible prosecution. Who better than Mrs. Challis, J.P., to have remembered that?"

"She'll get away with manslaughter," Kite said, "if they can prove provocation."

Provocation or not, she had killed. When she made that lunge for the knife, she intended to kill again—either herself or Challis. Mayo somehow didn't think that the length of her sentence was going to be the cross Gillian Challis would have to bear.

20

A few days later Edwin Saville sat in the back room at his shop, hunched over a pile of books in which he could summon no interest.

The bell rang as the shop door opened. Edwin sighed and didn't immediately stir. He was just rousing himself to answer it when Zoe came through. She'd brought teacakes again from the shop next door, the spicy ones he liked, crammed with currants and sultanas, to be served split and toasted and dripping with butter. It was becoming a daily routine with them.

There was a lot of confidence about her these days. Everything about her seemed more clearly defined—her hair was redder, her skin whiter, her eyes more green than blue. He knew, sadly, that she was glad Fleur was dead.

She thought, like everyone else, that he had been deceived by Fleur, taken in and touched by her glamour, as the rest of them were. She was wrong. His marriage to Fleur hadn't been perfect, but he had known her, through and through, and he'd loved her in spite of it . . . though he'd never been able to manage her. If he had, he'd never have allowed the quarrel that day to escalate; he'd have coped with things better, smoothed it over until she'd come to see the impossibilities of the situation, or until they could reach some compromise. But he'd never been very good at that sort of thing; it had always been easier, even with Margaret, his first wife, to give in. As he had when she'd insisted on going out in the boat that day, in rough weather with which he'd known he couldn't really cope. As he had with Zoe, too, agreeing to say nothing to the police about Michael's visit to the house on the day Fleur disappeared . . .

It was a hard thing for a father to have to admit he had believed his son capable of murder. It was part of the guilt he was going to have to live with. The other part lay in believing that Fleur would ever have left him for that Waterton chap. She would never have done it; he knew that now. She had needed him as much as he had needed her, perhaps more.

His shoulders sagged, his head rested slackly on the table. Zoe brought her own hand to lie next to it, the tips of her strong, thin fingers brushing his. There was suddenly uncertainty in the faint, closed smile on her lips, a question in her eyes. He stayed where he was, unmoving, and presently, when the silence became unbearable, she took her hand away.

ABOUT THE AUTHOR

MARJORIE ECCLES has written seven romance novels under two pseudonyms (Judith Bordill and Jennifer Hyde). This is her second novel for the Crime Club; her first crime novel was *Cast a Cold Eye*. She lives in Berkhamsted, England.